Dead Man's Bluff

Daniel Knott was a bad farmer and a worse husband. When a poacher heard a shot and shortly afterwards Knott's charred remains were found among the burnt-out farm buildings, the police felt they had not far to seek for the solution to the tragedy, especially when another body was found. It proved to be that of an agricultural salesman running a subsidy swindle in which Knott was deeply involved. And only the local Inspector Clayton was worried by the fact that the salesman had chosen to consume a dinner of boiled beef and dumplings on a sultry August afternoon. Superintendent Akers of the Yard was definitely not.

The poacher's evidence provided alibis for several suspects, but Clayton was not satisfied. When one of the alibis is broken and the suspect sent for trial, his dissatisfaction increases, but the results of his inquiries are unexpected, to say the least.

Roderic Jeffries spins one of his most intriguing mysteries, whose ramifications extend to include the kind of trial scene for which he is justly famous and a legal twist as cunning as any he has ever devised.

by the same author

A TRAITOR'S CRIME
A DEADLY MARRIAGE
DEATH IN THE COVERTS
DEAD AGAINST THE LAWYERS
AN EMBARRASSING DEATH
THE BENEFITS OF DEATH
EXHIBIT NO. THIRTEEN
EVIDENCE OF THE ACCUSED

Dead Man's Bluff

Roderic Jeffries

The Crime Club
14 St James's Place, London

ISBN 0 00 231174 7

© Roderic Jeffries, 1970

Printed in Great Britain
Collins Clear-Type Press
London and Glasgow

CHAPTER I

IT WAS a warm, sunny July, good enough to restore an Englishman's faith in the existence of summer. Daniel Knott walked up the pitted farm drive to the complex of brick-built, tile-roofed farm buildings which had once been the last word in modernization, but which in fifty years had become almost unworkable. He entered the dairy and propped open the lid of the bulk tank. Even before he read the dip-stick, he knew the quantity of milk was down because it reached less than half-way up the central paddle. The dip-stick gave a reading of one hundred and fourteen and he checked this reading on the wall chart. One hundred and seventy-six gallons. There should have been at least two hundred and fifty.

'Bloody old fool,' he said angrily.

He went through from the dairy into the herringbone parlour and stared with dislike at the two days' accumulation of slurry. When he'd inherited the farm and decided to become a farmer, he'd never considered he might have to deal with the muck himself: he'd never consciously connected muck with farming. He stared angrily at the control panel of the slurry disposal unit: that little lot had cost him over a thousand pounds and he could still remember how enthusiastic the farm manager had been about it until it was installed. It had never worked properly because too much straw became mixed up with the slurry. The manufacturers had told him that they could cure the problem for another two thousand pounds. He'd sacked the farm manager. Probably the man had had a rake-off from the manufacturers: most of the men who'd worked for him had proved to be crooked.

He looked at his watch and saw the time was eleven o'clock so the slurry would have to wait. If the cows didn't like it, that was their bad luck: when they gave as much milk as they ought to, he'd start to bother about their conditions. In any case, why hadn't the fool Browland cleared up? Browland ought to be sacked, but with him gone there'd be no one to milk the cows. Knott was quite certain he wasn't going to muck around doing that.

He left the buildings and walked back down the drive. Across the road, the cows were grazing the fourth paddock. Two of the paddocks should have been fertilized a couple of days back. He'd get around to them some time.

He went round the house to the back door and as the three dogs barked a greeting, he shouted at them to shut up. They quietened and flopped down on the concrete run with the listlessness of dogs who were never let out of their run.

The kitchen, an addition to the house which had originally been two cottages, had a flat roof which was always leaking. Months ago, Phyllis had asked him to get the builders to repair it. He went in to find she was trying to rake the Aga into life. She stood up and sweat rolled down her face. 'This won't work again,' she said, with angry resentment. 'The flue's all blocked up. I asked you to clear it.'

'And I told you I was too busy.'

'Doing what?'

He shrugged his shoulders and went from the kitchen into the smaller of the two sitting-rooms and through that to the hall and the steep stairs, which he climbed to his bedroom. He and Phyllis had slept in different rooms for a couple of years now. For some time after that arrangement had started he'd gone to her room at nights when his physical needs became great, but for all the pleasure she'd ever offered him he might as well have stayed in his own bed. He took off his overalls and carefully dropped them on to the floor. She would hate to find such untidiness.

He changed into a lightweight check suit. It was ironic to remember, he thought with angry bitterness, that when he'd first met her he'd found her coolness attractive. He'd been taken for a sucker: contrary to popular mythology, her coolness wasn't hiding anything other than large chunks of ice.

The dogs in the kennels began to bark once more. He leaned out of the open window and shouted at them to shut up. They looked up at him, then sank back on to the concrete that so badly needed washing down. They'd made a right Charlie out of him when he'd last been invited out shooting. The other guns were ignorant and didn't know a German Shorthaired Pointer from a Dalmatian: he'd told the guns how useless their fat old Labradors were when compared to his GSPs, which were faster, more obedient, had keener noses, and softer mouths. At the first stand a hare had come through ahead of the beaters. His three dogs had taken off after it. The hare doubled back through the line and the dogs followed, scattering the pheasants in all directions and ruining that drive. Eventually by a fluke, and in full sight of the head keeper, they'd cornered the hare, killed it, and eaten it. When he'd caught the dogs he'd thrashed them as hard as he could. One of the other guns, a pompous fool of a colonel, had told him to stop or he'd be reported to the RSPCA.

He crossed the room and looked in the mirror. Hazel was quite right, he didn't really look a day over thirty-five. Perhaps his hair was a little thin on top, but that meant nothing. When he was with Hazel, he didn't feel a day over twenty-five. By God, she knew why she was a woman! If Phyllis was an iceberg, Hazel was a volcano. It wasn't, he thought complacently, every man who could capture the love and affection of a woman almost half his age. Even to think of her was to excite his mind and trigger off memories.

He went down the stairs, carefully holding on to the rope rail because of their steepness. As the two cottages had once been for farm workers, safety demands or those of convenience had been ignored.

Phyllis was now washing up, as she so often was. Cleanliness and tidiness had become fetishes with her.

She turned and saw he had changed into a suit. Her mouth twisted into sullen lines. 'Are you going out again?'

'Yes.'

'I thought the vet was coming?'

'He is. The cow's in the collecting yard.'

'What happens if he wants help?'

'You're here.'

Her face suddenly crumpled and the sullen hate became pathetic defencelessness. 'Daniel . . . can't we do something?'

'About what?'

She flapped her hands. 'You know what I mean.'

'I wouldn't ask if I did.'

She washed a cup, so slowly and carefully it might have been a piece of Spode rather than chipped Woolworth. 'You're going to see that woman,' she said dully.

'I'm not going to see any woman.'

'Who is she?' Her voice rose. 'Why are you going out with her?'

'I'm not going out with any woman.'

'Is it the same one you were with at the restaurant?'

'How many times do I have to tell you that she . . .'

'She's only a girl, Daniel, she's only a girl.'

'She's the daughter of an old friend. But if she were what you keep saying she is, she'd at least have some red blood in her veins, not ice-cold water.'

'I can't help it if I . . . if I . . .'

'If you're a bloody sight colder than charity.' He was irrationally annoyed by the tears that began to well out of her eyes and he hurried outside, slamming the door shut behind himself. He went out of the garden and along to the tumbledown wooden garage. Inside was his Bentley.

Bought second-hand, five years ago, the body was now rusting in places and the oil consumption was high enough to show that something was pretty worn out in the engine, but it remained a Bentley and a man in a Bentley was a man of importance.

He backed the car out, turned, and drove down to the road. A small Austin went by and he recognized Mrs Mellish. Her father had been a war profiteer, yet she always referred to him as Knott the parvenu. It was a pity he'd never told the old bitch that there'd been Knotts at Knott Hall long before the days when her ancestors had swung from the gallows at Tyburn.

Phyllis Knott looked round the kitchen and reluctantly decided there was nothing left to clean or tidy. She went upstairs and into Daniel's room and found the filthy overalls which had been dumped on the floor. She knew they'd been left there deliberately, yet she still allowed them to infuriate her. Why didn't she take Elizabeth's advice and leave Daniel to go and live with Elizabeth?

She sat down on the edge of the bed. More and more she was drawn to the tragedy of looking back in time and remembering what things had been like when Daniel proposed to her. Life had been so wonderful. The Knotts were a county family, going back to the year dot and for her to marry one was, as her mother had said, a real feather in her cap. Some bedraggled feather! Not even a raving lunatic would call the home they lived in now one of England's historic country houses or describe her life as one of elegance and ease.

She stood up and crossed to the mirror over the dressing-table. She looked at her reflection. In a mood of bitter honesty, she saw a woman who was ageing fast, who had lost the attractiveness that had been hers when young, whose mouth suggested only discontent, bitterness, and a pathetic yearning for the unobtainable.

Her thoughts were interrupted by a hearty knock on the kitchen door. She went downstairs. It was the vet, a man whom she thoroughly disliked because of his unfailing familiarity.

'' 'Morning, Mrs Knott,' he said, 'how's tricks with you this lovely day?'

'The cow's in the collecting yard,' she answered coldly.

'Okeydokey. Is someone round to give me a hand?'

'My husband had to leave a short time ago on business so there's no one.'

'Then if there's no one available, I'll just have to try to do things on my own, won't I?'

He looked at the Aga in a way that suggested he would be open to an offer to drink a cup of coffee. She ignored him. He was so ignorant that he never dreamed of knocking on the front door, but he always came round to the back one—the first time he'd called, he'd caught her in curlers.

'How's the farm making out?' he asked, ignoring her cold hostility.

'Very well,' she lied.

'Churning out the milk, what? Except it all goes into the bulk tank.' He laughed immoderately.

'I must get on with my work.'

'I've just come from old Ampton's place—I suppose you've heard he's putting up another hundred and fifty kow kennels—expanding to five hundred cows. There's a go-ahead bloke for you and no mistake, but just think of the capital that that calls for!' He pursed his lips in a silent whistle.

She was convinced he was only telling her this in order to belittle the smallness of Knott Farm.

'Still,' he said, with brash loudness, 'he's a clever old boy —knows his farming from A to Z.' He ran a hand through his tight curly black hair. 'Right, Mrs Knott. I'll have a stab at the sick cow—with a hypodermic needle.' He left.

She went from the kitchen into the small sitting-room,

then through that into the larger sitting-room. When she saw how tattered and stained the carpet was, she felt like weeping. When they'd first come to the farm, Daniel had been all optimism. 'I know it's not a palace, but we'll soon knock it into shape. Those two sitting-rooms can be turned into one and we'll have a cocktail-bar—just a small one— over there . . .' Nothing had ever been done.

She sat down on the settee and lit a cigarette. They'd been at the farm for five years. For the first year, Daniel had oozed confidence. Farming was just like any other business and all the old hayseeds of local farmers, who spent their lives leaning on five-barred gates, were so stupid and bound by tradition that they couldn't hope to succeed in the modern age. On the other hand, a man who had vision, was clever, and possessed keen business acumen, must succeed. Some of Daniel's confidence, but none of his brash boasting, had disappeared during the second year. Now, by the fifth year, he was for ever blaming those same hayseeds of farmers for ruining him—without ever enumerating how they could be doing this.

He must have gone to see that tart of a girl again. Phyllis suffered both bitter anger and intense pain. How could he so lower himself and forget his heritage as to chase a slut half his age? How many of their acquaintances knew what he was doing?

Tom Browland cycled up the farm drive to the buildings and propped the bike against the outside wall of the dairy.

The cows were still out in the paddock, not in their lie-back field where they should be. He was not surprised. If Knott was anything of a farmer, he was a genius—and he knew himself to be generally considered simple.

He walked back down the farm drive with his feet, as always, splayed out. The village lads often imitated his walk, but that never worried him.

The Ayrshire cows were reluctant to leave the paddock,

but he had an endless patience that was not even upset when the large old white cow for the third time turned back and circled round behind him. He just plodded back to the end of the paddock and swore at the cow and she, as if worn down by his bovine patience, finally did what he wanted.

He took them up the drive and penned them in the collecting yard, then went into the dairy, checked the bulk tank plug was home, and started up the vacuum pump. He loved all this machinery, which had cost more money than he could ever really comprehend. He gained a great sense of importance from being in charge of it.

The bulk tank entry pipe needed a new filter and he fitted one. Then he left the dairy and went through to the parlour and down into the pit. He filled a bucket with warm water from the tap in the pit, opened the left-hand door and five cows came through into their standings, rumps towards him. He washed down their udders with warm water and disinfectant. He climbed out of the pit to feed them with crushed barley. On his return to the pit, he attached the five clusters. The milk began to spurt into the glass jars that were at head height. The rhythmic clicking of the pulsator, working off the vacuum line, gave him a conscious feeling of well-being.

CHAPTER II

AUGUST WAS a month of much sunshine and some of the local weather pundits began to prophesy a really hard winter—presumably on the grounds that bad must follow good. Tom Browland was unworried by past or future : his only concern was the present. He lived in a four-roomed cottage at the Cregiton end of the road which passed

Knott Farm. There was only cold water in the kitchen and sanitation was at its most primitive—an outside privy— yet he was perfectly content. The tenants of the council houses in Cregiton had hot running water and indoor flush lavatories, but their rent was almost three pounds a week whilst his was just over eight shillings.

He was a happy man. He was married, he had a kitchen garden in which he grew vegetables that invariably won prizes at the village flower shows, and beyond his garden and the rough field was Parson's Wood in which were quite a few pheasants.

Meg Browland was small and sharp and no one managed to pull the wool over her eyes. She hadn't, however, always been so sharp. When she was seventeen, one of the village lads had whispered so many sweet words to her that she'd offered up her virginity in a hay field with the greatest of pleasure. The pleasure continued for four months, at which time she became pregnant. On hearing the news, the father-to-be swore he'd never desert her. He then hurriedly left the village to go to work in London. She had a miscarriage. The other girls in the village—who somehow managed to escape pregnancy—scorned her and the boys reckoned she was fair game. One day she'd been almost raped in Parson's Wood and only Tom Browland's sudden appearance, on a poaching expedition, had saved her. A fortnight later, Browland offered her his largest cauliflower and a month after that he mumbled a proposal of marriage. She accepted him. She was sick and tired of being chased and although Browland was in many ways simple, she could be certain he would give her his unstinted love and affection.

On the twenty-first, eleven years but for a day after their marriage, Meg, who was clearing up the luncheon crockery, said: 'We ain't much to eat for tomorrow, Tom. D'you recollect it's our anniversary tomorrow?'

He grinned, his round face becoming creased.

'Can you find us something, Tom? It ain't right to sit down to nothing special on our anniversary.'

He fiddled with his large and bulbous nose, as he so often did when moved by some emotion.

'Fancy, eleven years!' She crossed the small kitchen and picked up her knitting—she was an expert knitter and sold her work to a shop in Gertfinden—and sat down on a chair by the table. 'Things 'ave changed a lot, Tom, 'aven't they?' She didn't wait for an answer. He was not a great talker and she had long since fallen into the habit of chatting on and on. 'Did you 'ear that Mary, from number four down the road, 'as been took to 'ospital? Collapsed, all of a sudden. I wonder what'll become of her kids if she goes—Alf won't look after 'em, that's for sure.'

He rubbed his nose again, looked through the window, and checked on the time. 'Ten past,' he said. He grinned slyly. 'I've time for a walk afore I goes back to milk.'

After leaving the house, he checked on the cabbage plants in the kitchen garden, then opened the small wooden gate and went into the field. This was part of Knott Farm, but being an outlying field it was totally neglected and the weed grasses, nettles, and thistles were so rampant that the dairy cows put out on it found little to graze. At the edge of the field, and separating it from Parson's Wood, was a dried-up stream and he scrambled across this and under the barbed-wire fence. He re-positioned the low-lying branch of an ash-tree so that there should be no mark of his passage—no keeper was employed on the estate now, but old habits died hard.

Meg wanted something special for the meal tomorrow, so she must have pheasant. The season for pheasants was a long way from starting, but only the rich worried about such things: a nice young cock bird—so long as it had almost matured to full plumage—tasted just as good in August as it would in October.

He had five feeding places in the southern end of

Parson's Wood and he kept these going throughout the year so that pheasants were always using them. An experienced keeper would soon have discovered them and known what they were, but others would not even notice them. He baited the first four feeding places.

He reached the fifth feeding place and took a handful of crushed barley from his pocket—part of the cows' ration for the morning—and was just about to scatter it when he heard a shot from relatively close by. He stood still and waited, fear twisting his stomach. There were often distant shots and the regular explosions of bird scarers when these were in use, but this shot had surely been fired on the estate. Poachers were never punished very hard, but he had an irrational fear of the law that was close to being terror. He took a battered five-shilling watch from his pocket and saw the time was five past three. Knott must be out with a gun and wandering round.

Instinct urged him to run, but Meg wanted a pheasant for the next day and if she'd asked for a slice of the moon he'd have done his best to get it for her. He waited a while, then scattered the corn. He moved slowly and carefully a hundred yards to the right and cut some finger-thick twigs from a hornbeam, using earth to darken the stubs on the tree. He stripped off all the leaves from the branches and pushed these down rabbit holes, cut the twigs into lengths ranging from eighteen inches to six, and with the aid of string fashioned a pyramid-shaped trap. As he worked, he listened carefully, fearing the sound that would send him bolting for safety.

He returned home and grinned at his wife, by which she knew they would have a celebration meal tomorrow.

Browland left his house and began to cycle towards the farm. The lane was narrow and by the entrance to the twelve-acre field it rose in a twisting hundred-foot climb which always brought him off his bicycle. When he reached the top he remounted and continued past the keeper's cottage, now empty and almost derelict. From here, he could see the farm buildings. Smoke was rising from the wing nearest the road and he wondered, without much real curiosity, what was burning.

CHAPTER III

DETECTIVE-INSPECTOR Jim Clayton leaned back in his chair and sighed. Who was it who dreamed up all the unnecessary paper-work that had to be dealt with day after day? He had the quick vision of a little man with a large head and horn-rimmed spectacles, racking his brain to think up new forms.

The telephone rang. 'You're not forgetting we're going out this evening, are you, Jim?' his wife asked.

'No, dear.'

'And you'll soon be coming home—it's quite a long drive?'

'I'm practically on my way.'

She sounded suspicious. 'You're quite sure?'

'I've never been more positive in my life.'

'Humph!' she said, and rang off.

He looked at his watch, then at the pile of forms still to be completed. They would have to wait for another day.

As he stood up, there was a quick knock on the door and Detective-Sergeant Morris came in. 'A report's just through of a bad fire at a farm at Endley Cross, sir.'

'How's that our pigeon?'

'There are two bodies involved.'

Only Morris would talk about bodies being involved in a fire, thought Clayton. 'Do we know anything more than that?'

'Nothing, sir, except that the fire became very fierce, very quickly. I've checked and there's no apparent reason for this.'

Morris never missed a chance, Clayton knew from experience, of pointing out how efficient he was. Tall, well-built, sharply featured, with a mouth that held a slightly bitter twist, he looked what he was—a man who admired only success and was determined to succeed at all costs. He had a dedicated ambition. Clayton had an inborn distrust of dedicated ambitions. 'I guess we'd better go and have a look.' He remembered the very recent call from his wife. 'I'll meet you down at my car.'

'Right, sir.'

Morris left and Clayton asked the switchboard operator for an outside line. He telephoned his wife. 'Margery, what time is the invitation . . .'

'Jim Clayton, are you about to try and cry off?'

'Something's turned up and I've got to slip out to Endley Cross and see what's what.'

'So help me, if you're not back here in time to drive over to Dawn's by six-thirty, I'll . . .'

He hastily interrupted. 'I'll be with you long before you can start to get fussed.' He rang off before she could point out that if he had to drive to Endley Cross, deal with the matter, and return to Gertfinden, he was hardly likely to be with her in time. Still, he tried to comfort himself, by now she was used to sudden upsets in plans.

His car, a rather battered Hillman on which he was given a poor mileage allowance when on police work, was parked in the courtyard at the back of the police station. Morris already sat in the front passenger seat. He started the engine, backed, and drove out on to the road, turning right.

'Who's out at the farm?' he asked, as he braked for Station Road.

'The local PC.'

B

'And who's he?'

'I've no idea,' said Morris, in a tone of voice which suggested that names of local PCs were unimportant.

Times had changed in the force, mused Clayton. Perhaps
this was good as well as inevitable, but that didn't mean he
welcomed it any the more—a sentiment that would have
aroused Morris's scorn. Yet surely there must be something
to be said for the time when there had been considerably
more contact between all ranks because communications had
been so much more primitive . . . Nor, he thought with a
quick grin, was he talking about fifty years ago, as some of
the youngsters might like to suggest.

The drive took them through south-east Gertfinden, a
shabby area in which were a large number of dilapidated
terrace houses that were only gradually being replaced by
modern council houses and also two industrial estates, only
half full because firms were still reluctant to set up factories
in the area.

Houses gave way to fields in which grass was browning
from lack of rain. When they turned by the garage, they left
the main road and drove along narrow lanes bordered on
both sides by thorn hedges, now uneven from the summer's
growth. Clayton loved the countryside for its air of unhurried peace. He was unashamedly the traditional copper,
looking forward to retirement among the hayseeds.

Knott Farm had lost all air of unhurried peace. Two
fire-engines were present, one in the drive, the other in the
field between the wing and the road. Between them, they'd
managed to contain the fire, but a portion of the wing had
been gutted and was now only a smouldering, smoking ruin
and wherever the jets from the hoses struck a hot enough
patch, a ball of steam briefly rose in sharp contrast to the
oily black smoke. Cars had stopped and a number of people
were watching. A patrol car had parked in the entrance to
the drive and two uniformed PCs were keeping the crowd
back and making certain cars were parked safely.

Clayton stopped by the patrol car, had a quick word with one of the PCs, then walked up the drive. He noticed that the post and rail fencing was in very dilapidated condition and the paddock between the drive and the road was thick with flowered thistles—two obvious signs of a farm in a run-down condition. At the back of his mind was the thought that at some time he'd read something about the owner of this place.

A uniformed PC came across from the fire-engine in the field to the gateway, the earth of which had been heavily ridged by the traffic of cows. ' 'Evening, sir.'

Clayton recognized the other, a man older than himself and almost on the point of retirement. 'Hullo, Lincoln—I didn't know you were out this way.'

'Been here for the past two years, sir.'

'The last time I saw you, you were doing a stint . . ?'

'Great Dering, sir.'

'That's right. We had a girl who'd disappeared, didn't we?—and we found her, much to her annoyance!' Clayton turned and spoke to Morris. 'OK, George, have a scout round.' The detective-sergeant walked off and Clayton spoke again to the PC. 'What have we got here, then?'

'Can't tell you much more than I reported, sir, on account of not being able to get too near the building yet. The firemen were called, but by the time they got here they couldn't save the section that's gone. When things were damped down a bit they could see the bodies inside and that's when they reported to Gertfinden, who sent me along.'

'What are the bodies like?'

'Pretty far gone, as far as I can tell.'

'Any idea who they are?'

'Not really, unless one of 'em's the owner.'

Clayton jerked his thumb in the direction of the farm-house. 'No one around to help?'

'No, sir, the place is empty.'

'Who's the owner?'

'Mr and Mrs Knott.'

'Of course!' No wonder the name of the farm had been familiar. 'Could one of the bodies be a woman's?'

'I don't think so, but it's impossible to be certain.'

'Who reported the fire?'

'Tom Browland, sir. He does a certain amount of work here. He came along for the afternoon milking, found the place on fire, and for once had the sense to break into the house and ring the fire brigade.'

'Why d'you say "for once"?'

'He's simple, sir, always has been. They say his father was over seventy when he was born.'

There was no one like the village PC for giving you all the details, thought Clayton. 'Where's he now?'

'Milking. That's what the humming noise is, if you can hear it over the row of the fire-engines.'

'Did he seem worried?'

'As soon as he was sure the fire was under control he said his cows needed milking so he was going to milk 'em.'

That possessed a simple logic which Clayton found satisfying. A countryman, simple or otherwise, would look after his animals as a first priority. 'Can he tell us anything useful?'

'I haven't questioned him, sir. Left that for you.'

Clayton thanked the PC and then walked closer to the building to speak to the station officer who was in charge of the fire-fighting. The station officer led the way along the side of the twelve-foot-high outer brick wall of the building to the collapsed section. Here, the heat engulfed them and Clayton felt the sweat spring out on his face and body.

The roof had collapsed on to the mass of flaming wreckage and as it had come down part had become wedged in such a way that it formed the top of a space some three feet deep: in this space could be seen the remains of two bodies.

Clayton stepped back until he was free from the worst of the heat. He took a handkerchief from his pocket and wiped the sweat from his face. 'What were things like when you arrived?'

'Very fierce.'

'More than you'd expect? After all, these old buildings have a lot of timber in them.'

'This wasn't just timber—at a guess, I'd say something like paraffin.'

'How long will it be before we can get to the bodies?'

The station officer pursed his lips. 'Could be quite a time yet.'

Clayton watched one of the hoses moved round to enable the jet to be played on to a different part of the smoking rubble. Only one thing was certain, he wouldn't be going anywhere with Margery tonight, so he must telephone her as soon as he could.

He walked back to the drive, then went past the next wing, in which he saw the dairy, to the main shed which he entered. Wooden cubicles lined each wall. Some of the uprights were broken and two of the sleepers which were the kerbs had been knocked out of true. There was slurry in the gangway that was now dried up into a hard mess, obviously there since the cows had been turned out to grass in April. He looked up. The roof was lined with tongue-and-groove boarding and the roof timbers appeared thick enough to support a palace. It really was a case of 'They don't build 'em like that these days.'

He walked down between the cubicles and half-way along was the entrance into the collecting yard where a number of cows were milling about in slurry inches deep. He carried on to the far doorway and beyond was a bay about fifteen feet deep and this led out on to a concrete raft on which was a feeding trough and about fifty kow kennels. He turned and studied the building to try and get an idea of the layout. Here was a massively built corn-store and interior Dutch barn, with walls twenty feet high and a tiled roof, which ran at right angles to the main shed so that the whole complex was like an E, but with one extra wing. However much had this lot cost to build—at a time when the pound was truly a pound?

A green half-ton van was parked on the feed-lot and on its side, in white lettering, was printed Louthy Feedstuffs. Morris, using a handkerchief, had opened the driving door and was peering inside. Clayton went up to him. 'Bit of an unfortunate name for a firm,' he said.

Morris stepped back and stood upright. 'Why, sir?'

'Very close to lousy, isn't it?' Morris did not smile and looked at him as if he had said something very stupid. He sighed. 'Is there anything inside?' he asked.

'There are some papers on the front seat and some sacks of something in the back.'

Clayton peered in through the open doorway. On the passenger seat were several long forms, clearly issued by the Ministry of Agriculture, and a small bundle of invoices. One of the dozen half-hundredweight paper sacks in the rear compartment was on its side and the printing said it contained magnesium-enriched cow cake. The odds must be that the driver of this van was one of the two dead persons. 'Dabs will have to go over this.'

'I'd already thought of that, sir.'

Morris would almost be bearable, thought Clayton gloomily, if only he weren't quite so certain of his own brilliance. He turned away from the van and studied the kow kennels, made from wood and corrugated iron. The two lines were at right angles to him, but through the mid-way gap of the nearer one he could see that the passageway had not been scraped clear of slurry since last used. This farm was in a far more slovenly state than he had first imagined.

He turned back. The interior Dutch barn had fifteen-foot-high entrance doors and these were jammed open because the steel overhead runners had partially broken away from the wall: the doors were almost bereft of paint and were badly rotted along the bottoms. He went into the Dutch barn. There was no hay there, but against the far wall were stacked a large number of paper sacks. When he went across to them and lifted down one from the top, he found it contained Louthy's magnesium-enriched cow cake. There must be quite a few tons there, he thought : at thirty pounds plus a ton, that was a lot of money to have lying idle, especially on a farm that appeared virtually bankrupt. He replaced the bag at the third attempt—his muscles were not as strong as he'd thought them. Ten feet from the nearest bags was a large green stain down the walls to show where water had been running over the years : some of the roof timbers showed obvious signs of rot.

He heard the crunch of regulation boots and PC Lincoln looked into the Dutch barn, saw him, and came inside. 'Sir.'

'Yes?'

'Mrs Knott has just arrived back home, sir. A friend drove her. She's in a bit of a state.'

'Thanks,' said Clayton. As always happened, he wished there were someone he could order to go and interview Mrs Knott, even while knowing there could be no one since it was his job to face her newly aroused misery. Because he had too much imagination and sense of compassion, he always immersed himself too deeply in another's grief.

He left the Dutch barn and shouted at Morris to have a word with the man who was doing the milking, then followed the PC along the drive round the side of the buildings, bordered on the other side by woods, past the main shed, the dairy, and the partially burned wing, and down to the house. He paused at the dilapidated wooden garage and looked inside. He saw a large grey car which he identified as a Bentley. Just beyond the garage was parked a blue Mini.

He went into the garden and knocked on the front door and immediately there was an outbreak of barking from the rear of the house. After a short wait, the door was opened by a heavily built woman whose main facial feature was a square, pugnacious chin, in the centre of which was a mole from which sprouted a large, curly black hair. She was dressed in a flower-patterned cotton frock which highlighted the dumpiness of her figure.

'What do you want?' she demanded in a deep voice.

'I'm Detective-Inspector Clayton. I'd like a word with Mrs Knott.'

'Well you can't come in. Phyllis is most terribly shocked.'

'May I know who you are?'

'I'm Miss Corrins, but what business of yours is that?'

He spoke pleasantly. 'I always like to know whom I'm talking to. I'm sorry, Miss Corrins, I'm afraid I have to have a word with Mrs Knott.' He couldn't name the precise reason, but something about this woman aroused in him an immediate and instinctive dislike and this was nothing to do with her abrupt, almost rude, manner.

She stared angrily at him, but finally stepped aside. 'You're not to forget she's very upset.'

He entered the house. 'I suppose you know there's no certainty yet that her husband is dead?'

'The constable said there were two bodies in the fire.'

'There are, but we haven't identified either body yet.'

'Why not?'

'We can't yet get to the bodies because of the fire,' he said patiently.

She spoke more loudly. 'I'll tell you one thing. If one of them *is* Daniel, it's good riddance to bad rubbish.' She stared challengingly at him, as if expecting some sort of outraged argument, but his expression did not alter and he said nothing. After a while, she led the way out of the box-like hall into the sitting-room.

Phyllis Knott was lying huddled in one of the two arm-chairs. Miss Corrins went over and put a hand on her shoulder. 'It's a detective, Phyllis. Now if you don't feel you can say anything, don't.'

Clayton studied Mrs Knott. Her face was slack and ugly from shock and her eyelids were swollen from tears, but he did not see the aching grief he sometimes had to face—yet experience had taught him how impossible it was correctly to interpret an expression. 'I'm very sorry to have to worry you,' he said formally.

She looked up at Miss Corrins in a mute appeal for comfort and the elder woman murmured something which Clayton did not catch.

'You've heard there are unfortunately two bodies in the fire,' he said. 'We haven't yet been able to get to them. Can you help us at all to identify them?'

She shook her head.

He asked her the next question with a deep and obvious sympathy. 'Do you know where your husband is?'

'No,' she answered, her voice muffled.

'When did you last see him?'

'He was . . . here when I left this morning.' Tears welled out of her eyes.

After a while, he said: 'What cars do you own?'

'Just the Bentley,' she murmured.

Miss Corrins spoke with loud belligerence. 'That's enough. You've upset her terribly.'

'I'm very sorry . . .' He stopped. How in the hell could one find words to comfort a woman who'd arrived home to discover she was probably a widow—even if her husband had possibly been a bit of a basket?

CHAPTER IV

THE POLICE DOCTOR was a rotund man with a round Pickwickian face and the kind of florid complexion that suggested either over-indulgence in good living or some degree of ill-health. He stepped clear of the jumbled mass of charred timber, broken bricks, tiles and glass, sat down, and struggled to get off the thigh boots which he had borrowed from one of the firemen. 'By God!' he said. 'It's still too hot for comfort in there.' Sweat trickled down his face and he impatiently brushed it away with the back of his hand.

Clayton took hold of the right boot and began to pull. 'Can you tell me anything yet, sir?'

'A little . . . Here, pull harder and I'll grab hold of the grass. These boots are like a bloody plaster, easier to get on than off.'

After a short while, they managed to remove both boots. The doctor put on his shoes and scrambled to his feet. 'Both bodies are badly burned and partially destroyed, but there's no doubt both are male.' He had a habit of speaking in short, hurried bursts. 'Not much left of parts of 'em, but the back of one head escaped too much damage : it's received a good belt from something.'

Clayton put his hands in his pocket and began to fiddle with some coins. 'Could it have been a falling beam?'

'I'm not going to be dogmatic at this stage, but I wouldn't think so. The position and shape of wound are wrong.'

'I've enough work on my plate without you turning up a murder,' said Clayton.

The doctor picked up his battered leather case. 'How's the wife?'

'Stunned, of course, but not completely grief-stricken. Perhaps she's still hoping against hope that her husband isn't one of the corpses.'

'Are there any chances he isn't?'

Clayton shook his head. 'I doubt it. His car is in the garage and he was at home when his wife left in the morning.'

The doctor looked around him. 'It's sad to see a place like this fall into such a state, isn't it? More especially if you knew it in the old days. My father used to get invited to some of the shoots here, even though he could hardly hit the proverbial hay-stack. That was when old Reginald Knott had it and the family still lived in the big house.'

Clayton looked across the road at the trees and massed rhododendron bushes which hid Knott Hall. 'Who lives there now?'

'I don't think anyone does. The place was hell to run without an army of servants and when Reginald Knott died they discovered it was riddled with worm, wet rot, dry rot, and anything else you can think of. I can remember the house being advertised for sale, but no one bought it. Still, we're told that's the cost of progress. Thank God I shan't live to see very much more of it.'

'That's being a bit pessimistic, isn't it, sir?'

The doctor smiled, with a trace of sadness. 'There's nothing like dealing with a lot of dead bodies to convince one of one's own mortality . . . All right, then? I'll be getting back home. You'll deal with the coroner, won't you?'

'Yes, sir.'

The doctor left, walking with a slightly rolling gait. Clayton took a pack of cigarettes from his pocket and lit one. He watched the firemen rolling up the hoses of the far fire-engine and wondered if the station officer's estimate was correct that in another hour all the debris would be cool enough for a thorough examination.

Morris came round the end of the building and along the hard-core road that ran by the side of it. To reach Clayton he had to cross some grass and he trod gingerly, as if worried about landing in some cow muck. Clayton suffered a childish hope that he would go sprawling.

'I've spoken to the cowman, Browland,' said Morris. His voice became angry. 'He's bloody stupid—couldn't get an ounce of sense out of him.'

'When did he last see Knott?'

'If you took any notice of what he said, he hasn't seen Knott for years.'

Clayton tapped the ash from his cigarette. He could just

imagine Morris's hasty impatience in the face of a simple countryman: Morris's world was the city and the wise-cracking villain. 'Where's this bloke Browland now?'

'I told him to hang on in case you wanted a word with him, but one of the PCs saw him slipping off through the woods after putting out the cows in the field.'

'Did you get any reaction from him when you said one of the dead blokes could be Knott?'

'For all the emotion he showed, I could've been telling him it rained yesterday.'

'That would have provoked far more, since it was fine all day.' As soon as he had spoken, Clayton realized Morris would fail to understand what on earth he was talking about. 'The police doctor says one of the dead men may have had his skull bashed in with a blunt instrument, so this is a murder case until we get contrary evidence. I want photos of the bodies from all angles before a single piece of the debris is touched, then photos of the buildings to give the general lay-out, and of the van. As good a sketch-map as possible and, if necessary, we'll call in the draughtsman tomorrow. Dabs to check the van sufficient for it to be driven to the station, then give it a thorough going-over. Get on to Bob or Abe at the station and tell him that although it's probably much too late, he's to try to make contact with Louthy Feedstuffs and find someone who can tell us who called here in the van.'

'Yes, sir,' said Morris, managing in just two words to suggest that all these orders were totally unnecessary since he would have seen to everything, no matter what.

Clayton turned and began to walk away.

'I suppose the pathologist has been called?' asked Morris.

'I'd think that's highly likely,' said Clayton, with mild sarcasm. He went back down the drive and spoke to one of the PCs from the patrol car. 'Get on to HQ on your blower and ask 'em to send out a pathologist.'

'Yes, sir.'

Clayton stared at all the people who patiently waited on the road. What were they really after? he wondered. Take them and show them the half-burned corpses and they'd be very, very sick.

The pathologist, a tall, lean man with an arrogant face, wore overalls, rubber boots, and rubber gloves. He had a habit of whistling as he worked, usually a cheerful waltz from some old musical comedy, making for a somewhat macabre contrast. From time to time he stopped whistling long enough to dictate to his secretary, an elderly, white-haired man with a heavy limp.

He stepped back over a pile of blackened bricks and studied the two corpses, which lay close to each other. 'I want a photo from here,' he said.

The detective-sergeant, photographic and finger-print expert, looked at Clayton. He had already taken photographs from that angle. Clayton, however, nodded. It was easier to take more photographs than to try to convince the pathologist that his wishes had already been exactly carried out.

The detective-sergeant, muttering to himself, set up the tripod, checked the flash equipment, and took two photographs.

'You can clear that rubbish away from the bodies, now,' said the pathologist. 'And make certain nothing lands on them.'

'That's a bit of a tall order, sir,' said Clayton.

The pathologist looked down his nose at such an impertinent observation.

Wearing overalls, gloves, and boots, two PCs and Detective-Constable Burrow, who had driven out from divisional HQ half an hour before, began the dirty and laborious job of clearing away the rubble from the bodies.

When the bodies were free, the undertaker's van—owned by the Gertfinden firm the police usually used in such circumstances—was driven to the end of the hard-core road. The two undertaker's assistants and the policemen carefully rolled the bodies on to plastic sheets which were then lifted on to stretchers. The stretchers were placed in the van, which drove away.

The pathologist stripped off boots and overalls and handed them to his secretary. He spoke to Clayton. 'I'll do the PM tomorrow morning at ten.'

'Right, sir.'

'Will you please have all available facts to hand, with special reference to teeth?'

'Yes, sir.'

'Good-night, then.' The pathologist strode off towards his car and his secretary followed, lurching from side to side because of his limp.

Clayton checked on the time: nine thirty-five. He returned to the burned-out section and made certain the searchers were taking samples of charred wood which were put in plastic containers that were numbered, with the numbers then entered on a sketch-map to show exactly where they had come from.

He left the farm buildings and walked down to the house. The Mini was still outside and the front door was opened by Miss Corrins. She was sharply antagonistic. 'Well—what do you want now?'

'To have a word or two more with Mrs Knott, if possible.'

'Certainly not. Her doctor's called and given her a strong sedative and in any case you've no right to bother her . . .'

'I'm afraid I have a job to do.'

She sniffed loudly.

'If I can't speak to her, would you answer a few questions?'

'Why?' she snapped.

He continued to speak in the same calm, friendly voice. 'I have to try to identify the bodies.'

She said nothing and he stepped inside. Openly indignant, but uncertain what to do, she hesitated, then led the way into the front sitting-room. She slumped down into an arm-chair and stared belligerently at him.

'Can you describe Mr Knott?' he asked. 'You know the sort of thing—height, age, weight, whether he'd any noticeable physical peculiarities? And d'you know if there are any photos of him around the house?'

She indicated the mantelpiece. 'There's a photo of him up there. God knows why!'

He walked over to the fireplace and studied the framed photograph. The man had a round, flattish face, slightly indrawn cheeks, thin lips, and a general expression of discontent. 'May I borrow this?' he asked.

She obviously wanted to refuse, but finally shrugged her shoulders. He slipped the photo into his coat pocket. 'How old is Mr Knott?'

'In his early forties. I don't know more exactly than that.'

'Can you give me an estimate of his height?'

'He's just under six feet. Used to be proud of his height— as if it were anything over which he'd control!' She snorted.

'Is he at all fat?'

'Not him. Herring-gutted, that's what he is.'

'Has he any physical peculiarities of any kind that you know of—scars, old wounds, that sort of thing?'

'I've no idea,' she snapped, 'of what his body looks like.'

He hadn't imagined they'd made a couple. 'D'you know if he's ever broken any bones?'

'I can't tell you.'

'Does he wear dentures?'

'He does and they click. If I were Phyllis, I wouldn't have him near me until he'd had something done about them.'

'There's probably a spare set in the house somewhere, isn't there?'

'I've no idea.'

'I'm sorry to keep on bothering you, but d'you think you

could have a quick look for me? It would be a tremendous help.'

She stood up, smoothed down the front of her dress which did so much to emphasise her lumpy ungainliness, and left.

He studied the room. It had about it the air of a place that wasn't really meant to be lived-in : nothing was out of place and even the pile of magazines had been squared up and placed exactly in the centre of a small wooden table. He had the mental image of two specks of dust meeting and celebrating wildly because now the continuance of the species was certain. The furniture and furnishings must once have been of good quality, but they now bore signs of heavy wear, the carpet was stained and almost threadbare, and the curtains were badly faded.

Miss Corrins returned to the room. She handed him with much distaste a paper bag and when he opened it he saw inside a set of dentures. They looked either funny or obscene and he couldn't really decide which. 'Many thanks,' he said.

'Daniel must be one of the dead men,' she said abruptly.

'Why d'you say that?'

'His car's in the garage. He wouldn't dream of leaving this place without going in that dirty big car which he's fool enough to think impresses people—as if they can't see it's all rusty and as if they didn't know what a hopeless failure he is.'

'Why didn't you like him?' he asked, using the past tense to refer to Knott because he had no doubt.

A strange expression, twisted, painful, defiant, crossed her face. 'No one liked him.'

'Why not?'

She sat down in the arm-chair she had previously occupied. Her dress rode up her legs to disclose a thick, flabby thigh. 'He was loud-mouthed, a boaster, and a fool. Look what he's done here.'

'How d'you mean?'

'He's ruined a good farm. This place used to have some

of the best grazing in the district. But what's it now? A jungle of thistles, nettles, and weed grasses. He hasn't dug out a ditch in years. It damn' well hurts to see a place get in such a state so quickly.' Her expression made it clear this was a genuine sentiment. 'Poor old Reggie who kept the place perfectly must be turning circles in his grave.' Her voice coarsened. 'But then there have always been two kinds of Knotts—the good ones and the bastards. When he inherited the place, he didn't know a Friesian from a Dexter, but to hear him talk you'd have thought he'd invented agriculture. He wouldn't take advice, wouldn't accept help . . . Still, Paul will change things.'

'Paul?'

'Phyllis's nephew.'

'Doesn't Mrs Knott inherit the farm?'

'Of course not. The estate is entailed through to the eldest male.' She spoke as if no other course was possible. 'I don't like Paul—too crude—but he's a real farmer. If anyone can get this place back on its feet, he will.'

He spoke curiously. 'You take a great deal of interest in farming, then?'

'I'd have liked to farm,' she said.

'So should I.'

Just for a moment, there was some sort of sympathy between them. This disappeared when she snapped: 'How ever much longer are you going to be before you tell Phyllis he's dead? You've no right to make her go on and on like this.'

'We're working as hard as we know how,' he said pacifically. 'There's one last question—when I came here earlier, you said that if Mr Knott were dead it would be good riddance to bad rubbish.'

'Well?'

'Had you any particular reason for saying that?'

'I happen to know the way he's treated Phyllis, that's the particular reason.'

C

'In what way has he treated her?'

'I'm not answering that question.'

He thanked her and left and returned to the farm buildings.

The clock below the high steeple of Gertfinden church was striking eleven when Clayton garaged his car. He let himself into the police house where he lived. The sitting-room was in darkness and he went upstairs. His wife was in bed, reading.

She looked at him. 'Fancy seeing you!' she said tartly.

'I know it's a bit late, but . . .'

'Jim Clayton, the very last word I had from you was that you'd quite definitely be back in time to drive me over to Dawn's for dinner. I've had to ring her and apologise and she says she'd arranged a very special meal.'

'Oh, lord!' he muttered.

'You really are the limit.'

'I remembered I had to telephone you and tell you I was delayed, but . . . To tell the truth, I forgot what it was I had to remember.'

'You're quite, quite impossible,' she said fondly. She had a pleasant face, not beautiful, but one which correctly gave the impression of loyalty and compassion. She loved her husband now just as much as when they were married nineteen years ago and although she had originally hoped and believed he would rise right to the top of his profession, she had long since become peacefully reconciled to the fact that he wouldn't because he lacked the thrusting ambition this would have needed.

He sat down on the edge of the bed. 'The incident I was called out to was a fire with two bodies and at the moment it looks like a murder case. One of the men was probably Daniel Knott.'

'Am I supposed to know him?'

'I couldn't place him immediately. He's from the Knott

family who've owned the same land out at Endley Cross from the year dot. The only time I've ever won a prize at school, it was one of the Knotts presented it to me.'

'You've never told me you actually won a prize at school!'

'It was when I was fairly young.' He leaned back until he was supporting himself on his elbows. 'He was a very tall and a very distinguished man with a beard and a monocle and he spoke like God. Much more terrifying than the headmaster. He must have been this bloke's grandfather.'

'Where do they live in Endley Cross?'

'It used to be Knott Hall, but apparently the big house has been abandoned. The present bloke's in what was probably the farm manager's cottage. He's made a right old mess of the farm and no mistake.'

'Who's the second dead man?'

'We don't know for certain, but it looks very much like an animal foodstuffs salesman.' He yawned. 'Is there any grub going?'

'I put some meat pie in the oven, but goodness only knows what that's like by now. I'll come down and cook you some eggs.'

'There's no need for you . . .'

'I'm not having you going to bed starving.' She climbed out of bed and put on a housecoat over her pyjamas.

He stood up and yawned again. 'I wonder what the special meal was that Dawn had prepared?'

'Knowing her standards of cooking, probably some over-done chops,' she replied, with the satisfied tones of a very good cook indeed.

CHAPTER V

THE NEXT MORNING, Clayton drove the mile to the central police station and arrived at eight-thirty. He parked his car in the courtyard and went inside, along the corridor, and up the stairs to his room.

It was a badly proportioned room, painted in a most depressing shade of brown, yet he had managed to invest it with some cheer. On his desk was a photo of Margery and another of his daughter, Brenda, who was in London training to be a nurse: on two of the walls he had hung some coloured prints of the Lake District, a part of the country he loved to visit. In the bookcase—large, Victorian, and made from mahogany—there were a number of text books and several old, bound volumes of *Punch* whose very dated jokes always amused him. Margery swore they were responsible for his sometimes appalling sense of humour.

He sat down and stared at the 'In' tray. Inevitably, the post had brought a further flood of paper-work: requests for witness statements, requests from the Alien's department, circulars and forms from county HQ . . . He pushed the tray to one side and took from his coat pocket the paper bag in which were the false teeth and laid it on the blotter.

There was a heavy knock on the door and Detective-Constable Pritchard entered. ' 'Morning, sir,' he said, in his booming voice.

' 'Morning, Bob.'

'HQ were shouting for you ten minutes back. Detective-Superintendent Barry wants a chat with you.'

'Right, thanks.'

'I'm still trying to get hold of someone from Louthy Foodstuffs, sir, but so far all I can raise is a night watchman who doesn't know anything about anybody.'

'Keep trying.'

'Will do.'

There was a refreshing boisterousness about Pritchard, thought Clayton; an impression of hard-fought rugger games and smutty songs roared out over pints of beer.

After Pritchard had gone out, Clayton rang the detective-superintendent at HQ.

''Morning, Jim. These two deaths—don't you think I should have known about them a lot earlier?'

'I got through to you last night as soon as I knew the facts, sir.'

'It was pretty late on, you know.'

Clayton shrugged his shoulders.

'If it's a murder case,' said Barry, 'we'll have to call in the Yard.'

'Surely, sir, there's no need . . .'

'Call 'em in smartly and their costs don't come on the county rates. We've always got to think of the money.'

'Why call them in at all?'

'A murder case collects a lot of publicity.'

'We can handle it perfectly well, whatever it collects.'

'I'm giving the orders and if the PM says murder, we call the Yard in, is that clear? I'm not having everything fouled up and the county force getting a load of stinking publicity.' He rang off.

Thanks a lot, thought Clayton, as he replaced the receiver. Barry was a man who had reached high rank in spite of himself and, having reached it, he spent most of his life terrified of making mistakes. Given the chance to shift responsibility, Barry jumped at it. In the present instance, long before anyone could be certain specialized help was needed, Barry was all but hammering on the doors of Scotland Yard for help, his one desire to make certain that if anything went wrong, he could not be blamed.

Clayton reached across for the 'In' tray and reluctantly sorted through the mail. After throwing a good half into the waste-paper basket, he returned the rest to the tray for attention at a later date. He went down to the divisional superintendent and made his daily report on the crime situation in the division.

He was back in his office and about to leave for the mortuary when Pritchard reported to him for the second time.

'I've at last got through to one of the managers of Louthy Products, sir—admitted he never reached the office before nine-thirty. Some job!' Pritchard laughed his deep, booming laugh. 'He says that their representative for this area is a bloke called Alexander. He lives in digs in Relstone and here's the address and telephone number.' He pushed across a sheet of paper.

Clayton read the address. 'Get on to that number and see if Alexander is about. If he isn't, I want a full description.' He pushed the papers across his desk.

'Roger, wilco, and out.'

Pritchard must have been watching an old RAF film on the TV, thought Clayton. 'Telephone me at the morgue as soon as you know something.' He walked across to the door, then stopped. 'How about the silver theft?'

'It's all safely in hand, sir.'

'What's that mean?'

'I told Sergeant Morris I'd had a word with the owner and got a list of the stolen silver. Sergeant Morris said he'd see the description was circulated to all the usual channels.'

'D'you think you could manage to remember to report to me before any definite action is taken?'

'No trouble at all, sir,' Pritchard assured him.

Clayton left his room, went downstairs, and out to his car in the courtyard. He drove across south Gertfinden to the morgue, an old and depressingly dirty building which had been scheduled for replacement for many years.

The PM room was far cleaner and better equipped than the rest of the place, thanks largely to the two pathologists who most frequently used it and who had threatened to refuse to work in it unless the walls were tiled, good working surfaces were installed, and they were given a rotating table and other essential equipment.

The post-mortem began at ten. The pathologist and the mortuary assistant were dressed in green rubber gloves and aprons, surgical hats, and wellingtons. The pathologist's secretary sat on a small stool and took down the dictated notes, while around the edge of the room a forensic scientist, the police photographer, the exhibits officer, and Clayton stood and waited.

Clayton hated PMs. It wasn't the actuality of the event that distressed him, but the fact that nothing else so utterly brought home the final degradation of death. He could never console himself with the thought that once he was dead he wouldn't give a damn what people did to his corpse.

'Inspector,' said the pathologist.

'Yes, sir.' Clayton moved away from the bench and stepped close to the dissecting table, now tilted, on which lay the remains of one of the charred bodies.

The pathologist held up an X-ray film that had just been developed. 'See this—there are several objects, probably metal, lodged in or near the backbone.'

Clayton stared at the X-ray film at the point where the pathologist's gloved finger pointed, but could make out nothing that held any significance for him.

The pathologist handed the X-ray to his secretary and then called for a large scalpel.

A uniformed PC looked into the room, saw Clayton, and used his hand to mime a telephone. Clayton went outside, into the warm sunshine.

'There's a message for you, sir, from Detective-Constable Pritchard. Alexander's landlady says he left his digs about half-past one yesterday afternoon and she hasn't seen him since. She's not been worried because he's often gone away for several days at a time.'

'Did Pritchard get a description?'

'Nothing of any use, sir. He says Detective-Sergeant Morris has said for him to go to the digs and speak to the landlady, but he knows you don't like him doing anything without your permission.'

Clayton could well imagine the coarse bellow of laughter that must have followed those last few words. 'Tell him to carry on to Relstone—but he's not to forget to clear himself with the divisional officer.'

'Right, sir.'

The constable returned into the building, using a doorway to the left of the PM room. Clayton lit a cigarette and smoked it, enjoying the added pleasure which came from knowing he ought to have returned immediately to the PM room. When he did go back, the pathologist spoke sharply. 'You've been gone a long time.'

'Sorry, sir. It was an important telephone call.'

The pathologist beckoned to his assistant, who passed across a small plastic bottle. 'This is what was lodged in the backbone,' said the pathologist.

Clayton took the bottle and opened the screw-lid. Inside were several tiny balls of lead, each one of which was flattened to a greater or lesser degree. 'Shot-gun pellets!' He looked up. 'But this isn't the body with the wound in the head.' As he spoke, he realized he would never make a more obvious remark. This body had virtually no head.

The pathologist resumed work. Clayton screwed back on the lid of the plastic bottle and handed the bottle to the exhibits officer.

The post-mortem was over. The forensic scientist, after signing the exhibits book, carried away in a large and battered suitcase a number of plastic jars containing specimens. The police photographer had a last word with Clayton, then left in a hurry because he was already overdue at county HQ at Relstone. The post-mortem assistant tidied up the second body, in so far as it could be tidied up, in readiness for replacing it in a chilled locker. The pathologist, helped by his secretary, stripped off gloves, apron, hat, and wellingtons, and washed carefully with a carbolic soap. When he'd dried himself, he spoke to Clayton. 'I suppose you want a quick report now, before I send in the usual written one?'

'If you wouldn't mind, sir.'

The pathologist took a cigarette-case from his pocket and helped himself to a cigarette. He did not think of offering one to his secretary or the DI. 'Both bodies are male, both lie within the age group of twenty-four to fifty. Body number one—the top half of which was virtually destroyed by fire—had been shot. He was dead before being attacked by the fire. He had an arthritic condition in the right hip—not very advanced. Height around six feet, but as with all estimates of height from bone lengths, there's room for a wide range of error. You have the dental plates found in his remains?'

'Yes, sir.'

'Body number two suffered equally extensive burning, although the site of maximum damage was different. Height about the same. He had suffered a heavy blow to the lower part of the back of his head, but the burn damage makes it impossible to say more than that it was probably caused by a blunt instrument about an inch in diameter. That blow was sufficient to kill him, yet there are signs of asphyxiation—some small haemorrhages on the lung surfaces—so that he must have lived after it. It's amazing what injuries the body will temporarily survive.' The pathologist rubbed his chin with his long, delicate fingers. 'There's a point of interest here—he was dead by the time the fire reached him. There are no smoke particles in the surviving air passages.'

Clayton, hot and stuffy, ran a finger round the inside of his collar. 'What does that add up to, sir?'

'Nothing definite. Since he was found face downwards, he could have fallen on to something soft that sculptured his face and prevented his breathing—he'd have been unconscious so there'd be no question of his being able to lift his face. His body was very extensively burned, but as happens even with external charring of this degree, the internal organs and body fluids have been remarkably well preserved. The contents of his organs and his body fluids will naturally want close investigation.'

'You've said it looked as if he'd had a meal of meat, dumplings, and greens?'

'That's right.'

Clayton spoke slowly. 'It's an odd meal to eat on a day as hot as yesterday was.'

The pathologist spoke briskly. 'Some people will eat anything, any time. I once knew a wealthy man who used to like strawberry jam with caviar. He died from Bright's Disease, which seemed a fitting end to such depravity.'

The story was lost on Clayton: he'd no idea what one should eat with caviar. He shut his notebook and slipped it into his pocket. 'Many thanks, sir. And if we could have the written report as soon as possible . . .'

'I'll do it when I can and not before,' snapped the pathologist. 'You've got the second man's dental plates?'

'Yes, sir.' Clayton tapped his left-hand coat pocket. 'I'm beginning to feel like a second-hand false teeth salesman.'

The pathologist glared at him, then hurried out. He left the PM room and returned outside to the warm sunshine. As he lit a cigarette, he wondered vaguely if he should try to cut down on his smoking as Margery was always trying to make him. As soon as the present case was over, he told himself.

He crossed the flagstoned courtyard to his car and as he sat down he checked the time. It was long past lunchtime and it now occurred to him that he had forgotten to tell Margery he might be delayed: he decided he'd not go home, but would have a quick snack at the police canteen.

The woman behind the counter in the canteen told him

lunches were served from twelve until two and after that they were not served : no one was going to make her work herself to an early grave. Clayton smiled, said he understood, but asked if there wasn't perhaps just one plate of something he could have to keep his ulcer at bay. He had a warm smile and the woman relented and brought him a plate of ham and egg pie and salad.

Returning to his office after lunch, he found four fresh crime reports on his desk : a smash-and-grab in west Gertfinden, two cars reported stolen from Westhurst, a case of vandalism in the main city park, and a minor assault at a village pub in Fallock. With the reports was a note from Morris to say that he was investigating the smash-and-grab, but had asked the uniformed branch to deal with the other three cases. As usual, Morris had taken the right steps. Clayton grinned. A most amazing man!

He telephoned county HQ and spoke to Barry.

'I've been expecting to hear from you all morning,' complained the detective-superintendent.

'The PM has only just been completed, sir.'

'All right, all right. So what's the verdict?'

'One of the men was shot and the other had been battered about the head.'

'Oh, my God!' moaned Barry. 'Have you identified them?'

'Not yet.'

'Why not? Why haven't you? How often do I have to tell you . . .'

Clayton noticed a large white spot on his right trouserleg and he tried to scratch it off with his thumbnail. He made a worse mess of things. Over the telephone, the complaints went on for a while, then Barry said that as it was now definitely murder he was applying to London for immediate help from the murder squad. Clayton tried again to argue against this action, but Barry was solely concerned with shifting the final responsibility from off his own shoulders. He cared nothing for the feelings and morale of the local divisional force.

Clayton yawned as he replaced the receiver. He had a vision of himself in a deckchair by the sea, a handkerchief over his face, sleeping peacefully. Regretfully, the vision vanished and he searched in his desk for the list of dentists in the division. He telephoned each practice, asking whether Daniel Knott was one of their patients, and his third call, by a coincidence to his own, proved successful. He said he'd be very grateful for some help from whichever partner had attended Daniel Knott.

The sunshine was hotter than ever. There was, he thought, a perverse meteorological law which ensured the hottest summer weather when he was most busy at work and the wettest summer weather when he was on holiday.

The drive was a short one and luckily he was able to park immediately opposite the three-storey Victorian house. He went inside and the receptionist, all glossy efficiency, took his name and crossed the hall to one of the rooms. While the door was open, he heard the shrill whine of a high-speed drill and he very carefully tried not to remember when he had last had a dental check-up.

The dentist was a middle-aged man with an elongated, mournful face which he held tilted to one side as if work had fixed it in this position. He led the way into a small sitting-room. 'How can I help you this time, Inspector?'

'You were Daniel Knott's dentist and I've brought you two sets of plates to see if you can identify them.'

'I read in the papers this morning there'd been a nasty fire at his farm and two bodies had been found—there was more than a hint it wasn't an accident.'

'It wasn't that. One of the bodies had been shot, the other clubbed, but that's as far as we know now.' Clayton took from his pocket the set of dentures found by the first body and the set Miss Corrins had given him. He handed them over.

The dentist examined them briefly. 'These are identical. I'll go and check with my records to make certain they're Knott's.' He was away a bare couple of minutes. 'They're his, all right.'

'Thanks a lot.' Clayton took the plates back and wrapped them up.

'Hell of a thing to happen,' muttered the dentist.

Detective-Constable Pritchard enjoyed life to the full. He liked his job reasonably well, never worried too deeply about it, and felt real animosity only towards villains who attacked old people or children. He played rugger for the police team, went to his local pub three evenings a week at least, and pursued women with cheerful vulgarity and a one-track ambition. His one deep regret in life was that he couldn't afford to buy an E-type Jaguar to burn up the roads.

After a quick courtesy word with A division duty inspector, to say he was in that division's territory, he drove from the central police station to the High Street, where a traffic jam held him up for almost ten minutes, and then out to Hammerton Road on the north-east side of the town. It was a residential road of rather poor semi-detacheds which looked as if they had been built between the wars. Only the small front gardens, mostly filled with flowers, gave any sense of colour and gayness.

As Pritchard knocked on the front door, he thought about the girl he'd met two nights ago in the pub : would she or wouldn't she? This difficult question was put to one side when the door was opened and a severe-looking, middle-aged, angular woman studied him with ever-growing disapproval. 'Well? What do you want?' she asked.

He introduced himself. 'I've come to find out what you can tell me about this bloke Alexander.'

'I suppose you'd better come in,' she said with obvious reluctance. 'Wipe your shoes carefully on the mat.'

Fancy choosing to live in a place where an old bitch like this was landlady, thought Pritchard. If a bloke couldn't go into a house without wiping his boots shiny, it wasn't worth going into.

The living-room was clean and bleakly tidy. He sat down on a chair and this squeaked noisily. From the look on her face, she expected it to collapse under him. He took out his notebook.

'What's happened to Mr Alexander?' she asked.

'We don't know yet.'

'But you think he may be dead?'

'Could be, Mrs Wade, could be.'

'He owes me some rent.'

Good luck to him, thought Pritchard. 'How long's he been with you?'

'He came here in March. My last gentleman had to move to the West Country and I advertised in the local paper. I told him I wanted a quiet lodger. He was that,' she added almost grudgingly.

'Where had he come from?'

'A place called Atherstone—he said it was near Birmingham. His wife died last year and he didn't want to stay in the district, so he moved south and got work with the firm that sold animal food. He said it was all right as a job : took him all over the place, which was what he wanted. Another thing, he's a sister at Parqueton and he can stay with her when he's working near there.'

'So he's not here every night?'

'He quite often isn't here. When he is, he maybe leaves early—says the farmers are early risers, so he's got to be one. Still, he's never no trouble. Never once woken me up, leaving early.'

'Can you give me the name and address of his sister?'

'That I can't. He just calls her Flo.'

'He must have mentioned her address at some time or another?'

'I don't spend my time gossiping with him,' she snapped.

And Alexander, thought Pritchard, certainly wouldn't want to spend his time gossiping with her. 'Do you know of any other relatives or friends?'

'No.'

'Did many people come and visit him here?'

'No, and he's never tried to bring back a chit of a girl as some of 'em does. I don't allow that.'

'Poor devils,' he said, without thinking.

She spoke angrily. 'What did you say?'

'Nothing, Mrs Wade, nothing.' He certainly didn't want a complaint laid against him—and this crabbed old woman looked as if she was more than capable of such a thing. 'Will you give me a description of Alexander—or better still, have you a photo of him?'

'Why should I have a photograph of him?'

He wiped some sweat from his brow with the back of his hand. He'd picked a Tartar and no mistake. 'What kind of bloke is he and what does he look like?'

'He's a gentleman.' She sniffed. 'You can't say that for many these days. Never a nasty word. Always opens the door for me.'

That, he told himself, was a load of wasted chivalry. 'Was he tall, short, thin, fat?'

She studied him. 'As tall as you and not nearly as fat.'

Pritchard, who prided himself on being solid muscle, became annoyed.

'He's nice curly brown hair and a neat moustache. He has a little trouble talking and his words are sometimes muffled. He's told me it was much worse when he was young.'

'How would you describe his face and complexion?'

She thought back. 'He's a round face, with nice fat cheeks. Got a sad look, but that's to be expected, isn't it? His complexion's a good colour, but then he works out-of-doors a lot.'

'Would you know if he wears false teeth?'

'He does, yes.'

Pritchard went on asking questions, but she was unable to give him a clearer picture of Alexander—for anybody, few things were more difficult to describe than physical appearance. He asked if he could see Alexander's bedroom and was taken upstairs to a room that was clinically neat and tidy.

In the wardrobe were a few clothes, including a suit and two pairs of shoes. Pritchard wrote down the size of the shoes, 11, not because he thought this could be important, but because Clayton, typically old-fashioned, insisted on every single detail being noted: he also wrote down the names on the labels of the shirts and the neck size. He crossed to the chest-of-drawers. In the top right-hand drawer were a couple of files filled with Louthy Products correspondence. Some letters were from clients, giving orders, some were from the firm to Alexander, and there was one from the Westminster Bank in East Relstone advising him that his account stood at just over a hundred and fifty pounds. Also in the drawer were two hand-written letters still in their envelopes, which were postmarked Atherstone, both from the same person Alice, both undated and without an address. The letters were full of the comings and goings of people both Alexander and the writer had known: Gert had had a baby, Joe had had an accident, Joan's daughter ought to get married quickly but wasn't going to . . .

He shut the drawer. Alexander had been lucky to have had a hundred and fifty quid in the bank. That was a hundred and fifty more than he had.

CHAPTER VI

CLAYTON STUDIED the papers which had come from the front seat of the van that had been at the back of the buildings at Knott Farm. Unless he were very much mistaken,

some sort of fiddle had been going on with fertilizer subsidies. Application forms for the subsidy were filled in by
the supplier and the farmer and then sent to the local
divisional office of the Ministry of Agriculture : the supplier
gave his trading address, the amount of fertilizer supplied,
an analysis, the amount paid, and he signed a declaration,
while the farmer gave his name and address, his farm
holding number, and he signed a declaration that he had
received the fertilizer and used it for proper agricultural
purposes. Subsidies paid ranged from a pound or two a ton
on basic slag to over ten pounds on compound fertilizer.
There had been twelve forms in the van, filled in but dupli-
cated, with the second one in each case for more fertilizer
than the first. Clayton compared two forms. On the first
the farmer, East, had received five tons of compound fertilizer, on the second, ten tons : on the first the supplier's
name was stamped with a rubber stamp, on the second it
was typewritten : on the first the supplier's signature—
Hatchard—was clear, on the second it was an illegible
scrawl.

Clayton leaned back in his chair. The workings of the
fiddle were clear. Alexander would collect one form from
his firm, then hand the second one to the farmer, who
would send it on to the Ministry. The subsidy would be paid
on double the tonnage actually received and Alexander and
the farmer would split the extra. The chances of discovery
were very slim—the Ministry was unable to do much cross-
checking, being as snowed under with unnecessary work as
any other bureaucratic institution.

The odds were, of course, that here was the motive for
murder : an arrangement for a swindle which classically
ended in one swindler trying to swindle the other. Probably
Knott had previously applied for and been given the subsidy
on double the amount of fertilizer supplied and then when
Alexander had come for his half of the extra Knott had
refused to pay anything, secure in the knowledge that Alex-

D

ander wouldn't dare report him. Furious, Alexander had reached for the nearest weapon, an iron bar or a solid wooden billet . . .

The telephone interrupted his thoughts. The switchboard operator said it was an outside call from the Riverside Insurance Company.

'My name's Miller and I'm the manager of the Parqueton branch. Sorry to bother you, Inspector, but I'm hoping you'll be able to help me.'

'What's the trouble?' asked Clayton.

'Can you say whether or not Daniel Knott is dead? I see from the papers there's been a fire on his farm and two bodies have been recovered from it.'

'It's fair to say there's been a positive identification of him, yes. How does that affect you?'

'Very heavily,' said Miller wryly. 'He held life insurance for forty thousand.'

Clayton whistled.

'What killed him? From the way the papers reported things, it seemed you might be suspicious.'

'He was shot in the stomach. Alexander, the second man, was battered on the head with something solid.'

'Ye gods! Inspector, the beneficiary of the life insurance is Hazel Clews.'

'Not his wife?' Clayton began to tap on his desk with his fingers. 'Who's Hazel Clews?'

'I can't tell you any more than that her address is five, Dock Road, Trighton-on-Sea.'

'I'll just make a note of that.' Clayton wrote down the address.

'We naturally always have a close look at large policies, Inspector. Since Knott only took this one out six months ago, we're obviously wondering whether there's any chance of fraud here?'

'I can't answer that one yet,' replied Clayton. 'But if it was fraud, he went to unusual lengths to perpetrate it.'

'Quite so,' replied the other, finding the comment in poor taste. 'D'you mind if I keep in touch with you?'

'Of course not.'

Clayton replaced the receiver. Forty thousand pounds was a great deal of money, even in days of government-inspired inflation. He picked up the internal telephone and dialled the detective sergeant's room. 'Drop everything, George, and get over to No. 5, Dock Road, Trighton and . . .'

'I'm pretty busy, sir.'

'You're even busier, now. Find out who Hazel Clews is, what she's like, and what her relationship to Knott was.'

Detective Sergeant Morris swore as the CID Hillman slowed down on the steep, curling hill out of Abbotsbridge and a Mini drew out and passed. He hated being passed.

Eventually the Hillman struggled to the crest of the hill. It gathered speed and began the six-mile descent into Trighton-on-Sea. Morris used his left hand to take a pack of cigarettes out of his pocket and light one. He passed the caravan camp, which was sited on top of the cliffs and had a magnificent view across the sea, and he thought about his wife. It still hurt to remember her, even though he always said to others that when she cleared out of the house he had begun to breathe again. She'd a hell of a will and was as stubborn as a mule—time after time, she'd refused to do as he wanted on the grounds that she might be married to him but that didn't mean she had to subjugate her will to his. Did she now go around with other men? He gripped the steering-wheel harder. If ever he found her out with another man, he'd smash the bastard into pulp.

Trighton-on-Sea was a busy port, a large shopping centre, and on the outskirts was a growing amount of light industry. The old town to the east was a place of narrow, twisting roads and half-timbered shops and houses, and it contained several antique shops whose prices were fixed to tourists and foreigners: the new town to the north and west was a functional but ugly conglomeration of housing estates, supermarkets, and chain stores. The docks had been modernized and new facilities installed for Continental traffic, both passenger and cargo. Immediately about the docks had been a slum area, but now much had been re-built to modern standards. Dock Road ran parallel with the sea and number five was near the eastern end of the docks. Morris knocked on the door and this was opened by a blonde who was the sexiest woman he had seen for a very long time. 'Miss Clews?' he asked.

'Well?' she answered.

He introduced himself. Daniel Knott must have led a busy life with her, he thought.

Clayton looked up at the station clock. The train was already ten minutes late but, by British Rails' standards, it could be said that it was not yet really due.

He began to pace the platform. Was there any chance now of his being able to start his holiday on time? Margery had wanted to go to Jersey and they'd booked at a hotel which had been recommended to him by the DI of B division. It was an expensive place and he wasn't certain they were justified in spending so much, but he'd said nothing to Margery because they hadn't been abroad since their honeymoon.

The train came round the curve and pulled up at the platform with a slight squeal of brakes. Because it was relatively late, not many people left it and he identified the two from Scotland Yard immediately. He went up to them. 'Superintendent Akers?'

'Yes.'

'I'm Clayton, sir.'

'How d'you do. This is Sergeant Bodmin.'

Akers, thought Clayton regretfully, looked what reputation named him—a real thrusting go-getter. He had a long, narrow face with very sharp features and a pugnacious chin. His black hair was sleeked down, his suit fitted him in a costly fashion, and his shoes were brightly polished. 'I've got my car outside,' said Clayton. 'I'll take you to the hotel. It's a nice place, just off the High Street . . .'

Akers interrupted him. 'It'll be best if we go straight out to the farm. You can give me a résumé of the facts on the journey.'

'Right, sir. But what about dinner? I'm afraid that they stop serving at nine—you know what country hotels . . .'

'We had sandwiches on the way down.'

Something about the detective-sergeant's expression caught Clayton's attention. Bodmin, a square man with unusually large ears, had a hungry look about him, as if the sandwiches had not been very filling.

Clayton led the way to his car. After stowing their suitcases in the boot, he drove out of the car-park and braked to a halt as he waited for a stream of traffic to pass.

'By the way, when's the next press conference?' asked Akers.

'I haven't really fixed one, sir.' The road became clear and Clayton turned left. 'The London papers are still working through their local correspondents, so there's not all that much pressure.'

'The London papers are likely to send reporters down when they know I've been put in charge of the case, so you'd better arrange a press conference for ten o'clock each morning unless I tell you to the contrary.' Akers paused, then said : 'It pays, Inspector, to work with the press.'

'Yes, sir.'

Akers took a pipe and a pouch from his pocket. He filled the pipe with tobacco and tamped it down with a forefinger. 'You can give me the facts now—and don't bother with any extraneous details.'

Clayton gave him the facts.

Akers lit his pipe. Although the car windows were open,

the car filled with foul-smelling smoke. 'This half-witted cow-man—surely he can fill in some of the details?'

'I'm hoping he can, sir.'

'Then you haven't tackled him yet?'

'Not yet. I wanted to get the broad background first.'

'A case becomes a matter of priorities,' said Akers, in a tone of voice which plainly declared that broad backgrounds were not priority number one.

They reached the countryside, now disappearing behind the gathering darkness but, as it did so, gaining a strange, eerie beauty because a mist was rising and lying in streaks which cut off trees from their bases and animals from their legs. When they came to the ruins of Malmster Castle, on the hill to the right of the road, Clayton said : 'That's rather attractive in these conditions, isn't it, sir? Malmster Castle was sacked in the Civil War.'

'Really?'

'The Royalists had been besieged for almost a month and no one could get any supplies through until a woman . . .'

'How strong's the identification of Knott?' demanded Akers.

Clayton jerked his mind away from the Royalists, desperately holding out, and the woman who had sacrificed her most precious possession—as the chronicles delicately put it —in order to smuggle food and arms to the besieged. 'The false teeth were his. The doctor has confirmed that he had complained of pain in his right hip, although no conclusive diagnosis of an arthritic condition had been made. He was lying on his back and although he was so terribly burned a little of his clothing, protected by his buttocks, survived : there were the remains of green overalls, grey flannel trousers, and red patterned pants. His wife confirms that's what he was wearing when she left in the morning.'

'Then it's virtually conclusive.'

'Yes, sir.'

'How is his wife?'

'She's still shocked, but it's difficult to say whether it's his death, or what, that's shocked her. One thing's pretty clear, the marriage had long since ceased to mean much.'

'Did she know about this girl, Clews?'

'I haven't questioned her on that point, sir.'

'Oh! I'd have said it was rather an important one. What kind of family are the Knotts?'

'They used to be what was called county—owned a hell of a lot of land. I suppose at one time they must have been the biggest landowners for miles. They really got going just after the Civil War because when Malmster Castle fell . . .'

'I think we can skip the history, Inspector.'

It was strange, mused Clayton, how few people now were interested in the past. Yet surely . . .?

'Well?' snapped Akers. 'Let's hear what kind of a family they are now.'

'The estate's shrunk to a farm of about a hundred and seventy acres and a couple of hundred acres of pretty useless wood. Daniel Knott's father seems to have been a good farmer, but Daniel Knott was quite hopeless—the place has fallen into a terrible state. I gather there's an odd fact about the Knotts—they come in two very distinct types : one kind's clever, industrious, hard-working, the other kind's lazy, self-opinionated, and stupid.'

'What's the wife's background?'

'As far as I can make out, she comes from a small shop-owning family. When she married Knott she must have reckoned she was jumping up the success ladder and she's become soured as the ladder crumbled. He was a cocoa-broker in the City until he inherited the estate. When he came down here his loudly professed aim was to show all the locals what lousy farmers they were.'

'Your report said the farm passes on to a nephew?'

'I've been told it's entailed through to Paul Hulton, who's the only son of Daniel Knott's sister.'

'And does the wife get nothing?'

'A valuation of what's on the farm, I suppose, but beyond that there can't be much to have.'

Clayton turned off the lane they were on and into another which went up a slight hill and then twisted and turned in characteristic fashion as if seeking the longest distance between two points. He switched on the headlights and almost immediately a bird flashed through the right-hand beam, skimming the road by less than a foot. He wondered what it was. Fifteen years ago he would have identified it as a sparrow-hawk, but now they were virtually extinct in this part of the country. There had been far more changes in the countryside than most people realized, nor did they begin to acknowledge that these changes had come about because they demanded a policy of cheap food : rabbits had been decimated by myxomatosis, birds of prey had almost vanished because of the use of farm chemicals, more and more hedges and woods were grubbed up to provide arable land, few chickens were to be seen outside scratching happily in the dust, calves were turned into veal without their ever being in daylight, cows were zero-grazed and never stepped off concrete . . .

They reached Endley Cross and Knott Farm. Clayton parked the car in front of the house. He reached into the glove locker for a torch. 'Where d'you want to start, sir?'

'We'll have a look at the buildings. After that, I want a word with Mrs Knott and the cow-man.'

Clayton looked at his watch. 'He could be asleep by then, sir.'

'Asleep?' said Akers, in tones of disbelief.

'He'll have to be up by five each morning to milk the cows.'

Akers looked as if it had never before occurred to him that someone had to milk cows in the early morning. 'All right,' he muttered, in tones of annoyance, 'we'll see him first.'

'I'll just go in and tell Mrs Knott we're here. See you

by the buildings, sir. The burned-out section is on the right.'

Clayton opened the broken-down garden gate and walked up to the front door. The dogs at the back began to bark furiously. He knocked and waited, but there was no reply. After a second knock, he went to the garage and found the Bentley was out. He gained some small pleasure from the fact that things weren't arranging themselves as Akers had decided they should.

He went up to the buildings to find Akers, outside the dairy, talking to a powerfully-built man in his early thirties. Bodmin stood to one side, his heavy face showing little expression.

'Paul Hulton,' said Akers.

Clayton studied Hulton as well as he could in the growing darkness. Hulton was dressed in dungarees and a coarse blue shirt, both stained with dried dung. He had the build of a really strong man and a broad face, with lines of bitter, dogged defiance. His mouth was generous and his lower lip curled over. His eyes were a deep brown.

'He couldn't wait to get his hands on this place,' said Akers sarcastically.

'A farm doesn't stop when you tell it to,' replied Hulton scornfully. 'Animals don't work a forty-hour week.'

'Does Mrs Knott know you're here?'

'I saw her earlier on.'

'Did she ask you why you hadn't waited until her husband's bones were cold?'

'Look, Mister, this place is mine. For five years I've seen it being ruined by that bloody old fool. I don't give a damn what state his bones are in. Farm! He couldn't grow a rotten potato.'

'But you reckon you can?' Akers could not hide his anger at the cavalier way in which he was being treated.

Hulton spoke with greater contempt. 'Of course I can. I was getting a hundred gallons a lactation more than anyone else would from the broken-down herd I had.'

Clayton spoke quietly. 'Do you own the farm where you've been?' Hulton swung round and Clayton could not miss the look of hatred in his eyes.

'It belongs to a dried-up bastard called Fingle. I was called farm manager. I'll tell you what there was to manage. Forty scrub cows, chucked out from other people's herds and riddled with mastitis, bucket milking, an old shed that was alive with disease, paddocks thick with weed grass, and me not allowed to use a pound of basic slag or nitrogen . . . I'll tell you something more and you won't believe it. This place is a model farm compared to that.'

'Have you left there?'

'I quit. I told the bloody old fool what he could do with his farm.'

'When?' snapped Akers.

'The moment I read Daniel was dead.'

'We're not yet certain he is dead,' he lied.

'Phyllis said he was dead. The papers said he was dead.'

'The papers merely said that two bodies had been found in the debris.'

Hulton rested his thick, massive hands on his hips. 'Then come on and tell me—is he dead or isn't he? You must bloody know by now.'

'You'll have to go on waiting before you can be certain whether all this is yours, or not,' said Akers with malicious pleasure.

Hulton swung round, slammed open the sliding door of the dairy, and went inside.

Akers led the way along the earth drive which went round the west side of the buildings. 'He's in a goddam hurry to take over.'

'Somewhat understandably, sir,' said Clayton.

'Quite!' replied Akers.

'I didn't mean from any ulterior motive, but simply because he's obviously a genuine farmer at heart and so he'd have suffered at seeing this place become derelict. You know, a real farmer has a love for soil and stock, which means he hates seeing a place go backwards—of course, when he's due to inherit it and remembers the old saying that one year's neglect means five years' thistles . . .'

'You sound like the Archers,' said Akers, and it seemed he could offer no greater insult.

They continued in silence until they reached the concrete raft on which were the kow kennels.

'The van was there,' said Clayton, pointing to a spot in front of the interior Dutch barn.

'You haven't marked the position.'

'No, sir, I didn't think it necessary. I had an accurate sketch-map made and we took a number of photos . . .'

'You should have marked the position.'

Black marks galore, thought Clayton, and a dunce's cap. He smiled at the thought of himself in a dunce's cap, but stopped smiling when he saw that Bodmin was watching him.

Clayton switched on the torch and stepped over to the doorway of the Dutch barn. He shone the beam inside. 'There are two odd things, sir. First, there's no hay or silage on the place.'

'So what?'

'You must have winter feed unless you're going to buy in everything and then you need enough cows to make that economically feasible.'

'You told me the place was derelict. It's obvious he didn't give a damn about the winter. What's the other thing?'

'All that cow cake over there.'

Akers stared briefly at the paper sacks. 'One minute you're complaining because the cows haven't any food, the next you're complaining because they have.'

'But you don't need much cake at this time of the year. The grass obviously isn't as nutritious as in May or June, but it's still good for maintenance and a gallon, maybe a little more . . .'

Akers spoke impatiently. 'For God's sake, Inspector, forget the dietary needs of cows and start concentrating on things that matter.'

Clayton switched off the torch. 'Very good, sir.'

Akers led the way to the end of the concrete float and down the side of the east wing to the hard-core road and the burned-out section. He demanded the torch, switched it on, and shone the beam over the debris. 'This will all have to be sifted through.'

'I've had it searched, sir.'

'And I'll have it searched again,' snapped Akers. He clearly wanted the job done properly. 'Bodmin, see to it tomorrow morning. Tell the inspector the number of men you want and make certain they sift every last ounce of stuff.'

'Yes, sir,' said Bodmin.

Akers walked on round the end of the wing and then back to the passageway between that wing and the dairy. There was a light on next to the dairy and he continued along the passage until he could look through a window. 'What the hell's that?' he asked.

Clayton went up to his side. 'The parlour, sir. That's where the cows are milked.' Hulton was stripping down the rubbers of one of the claws and judging from his expression the rubbers were either perished or extremely filthy.

'What a hell of a contraption for getting some milk out of a cow,' said Akers, puzzled.

'It's a herringbone, said to be the best kind of parlour for a biggish herd. The cows come in batches on either side and stick their heads . . .'

'I'm as interested in the mechanics of milking as I am in the cows' dietary requirements.' Akers turned round and crossed the passage.

From the south end of the east wing to the point at which the fire damage began—and where an internal wall had collapsed at the top—was a feed store: a circular wire silo, containing barley, was in one corner and from this an auger led up to a mill: below the spout of the mill was a small heap of crushed barley. Dirt was thick everywhere and there was a strong smell of mice: dozens of empty paper sacks lay untidily about the floor.

'Where did the gun come from?' demanded Akers suddenly.

'I haven't discovered yet, sir.'

'Don't you think that's a matter of some importance?'

Hell, thought Clayton, the case wasn't thirty hours old yet: if he'd been able to find out all the answers to all the questions already, he could have taken over the chief constable's job. His stomach suddenly gurgled, reminding him how hungry he was. Stupidly, he hadn't eaten before meeting them, relying on driving them to their hotel and then hurrying straight home for dinner. Margery had said she was preparing liver and bacon and this was a dish he really liked. His stomach gurgled a second time.

Akers suddenly crossed to the doorway. 'All right, we'd better go and see this cow-man—if he hasn't already gone to bed because the sun's disappeared.'

Akers, on the short drive to Browland's cottage, asked how soon the men could start searching the rubble the next morning. Clayton suggested eight o'clock. Akers said that as it was light by seven-thirty, that's when they'd start.

The door of the cottage was opened by Browland. He was wearing a collarless shirt and patched trousers held up by ragged braces. When he saw Clayton and learned who Akers was, his fear was immediate and obvious. He stood in the doorway, speechless, and it was Meg who asked them into the sitting-room. Clayton spoke quietly to Browland, trying to calm his fears, and as he did so he became more and more aware of a rich smell of cooking.

Akers stood in front of the empty fireplace and there was an expression of distaste on his sharp, angular face as he looked round the badly furnished room. 'You've made a statement and I want to check it.'

Browland cringed. 'I don't know nothing.' Meg tried to smile encouragement at him.

'Come on, man, buck your ideas up : this is a very serious case.'

'I don't know nothing.'

'Just tell the gentlemen what happened,' said Meg softly. 'You were going to the farm and saw all the smoke and the flames.'

'There was all the smoke and the flames,' said Browland stupidly. He fiddled with his nose and his very light eyes seldom looked away from his wife.

'What happened then?'

'I cycled and saw the fire.' He fiddled harder with his nose. 'There weren't no one at 'ome so I got in and telephoned.'

'You didn't see a single person?'

'There weren't no one to see.'

'When had you last seen Daniel Knott?'

'After I finished milking in the mornin'. 'E tells me to clean up the collecting yard. I says I couldn't.'

'Why not?'

'I 'ad to come 'ome.'

'Why?'

Browland looked pathetically at his wife.

'Why should 'e clean up?' she demanded in a shrill voice. ''E weren't paid for doin' anything but milk the cows—and 'e weren't paid proper for doin' that.'

Akers took his pipe from his pocket. He lit it, not bothering to ask permission to do so. 'What was in the part of the building that's burned down?'

'Things.'

'Goddammit, what kind of things?'

Browland licked his lips. He fiddled still harder with his nose.

'What was in that part of the buildings?' demanded Akers, with loud exasperation.

'Tell 'im, Tom,' said Meg. ' 'E only wants to know what Mr Knott kept there.'

Browland took a deep breath. 'Diesel oil what was for the tractor, paraffin for the stove, buckets what we used for calves.'

'Nothing else?'

Browland nodded.

'Then what was there?'

'There was spares for the tractor and . . . and the old fertilizer spinner what wouldn't work and the deep-freeze what he kept the dogs' food in, and some shovels.' His wide brow became furrowed. 'There were a dung fork—or were that round the corner?' He shook his head. 'I can't rightly remember.'

'Never mind, Tom,' she said, 'you're doing real good.'

He was heartened by her praise. 'Then there were the old gun what 'e kept in the corner . . .'

'What old gun?' snapped Akers.

Browland was frightened by the other's tone of voice. He moved closer to his wife.

Clayton cut across what Akers had been about to say. 'Was this some old shotgun, just about falling apart? There's usually one on every farm?'

Browland looked quickly at Clayton, then back at his wife. 'It weren't that bad. 'E used it for rabbits, them what myxy didn't get. 'Course, 'e'd got a good gun for when 'e went shooting proper.'

'And did he keep any cartridges out by the gun?'

'There was always some. Up on the old shelf.'

'Were there any there yesterday morning?'

Browland slowly shook his head. 'I can't rightly remember seein' 'em, but there were always some there.'

'Was he a good shot?'

Browland sniggered. 'I see 'im miss a rabbit what sat and

looked at 'im not twenty yard away. 'E didn't 'alf swear 'cause 'e was always sayin' what a good shot 'e was, never missed nothing. Missed that rabbit and no mistake.'

'Can't you remember if there were any cartridges on that shelf in the morning?' snapped Akers, angry at being ignored.

Browland again became frightened. He fingered his nose as he looked anxiously at his wife.

Akers swore under his breath, had a last contemptuous look round the ill-furnished room, then led the way out. Clayton thanked the Browlands.

As he sat down in the front passenger-seat of the car, Akers said disgustedly : 'He's utterly useless as a witness— talk about the village idiot!'

'Don't you ever have idiots in town, sir?' asked Clayton.

Akers ignored the question. Clayton tried to start the engine and it refused to fire. To be marooned outside Browland's cottage was all that was needed to complete the evening, he thought gloomily. Luckily, at the third attempt he started the engine.

CHAPTER VII

CLAYTON AWOKE and saw it was late. He washed and dressed and hurried downstairs to the kitchen, where Margery was cooking breakfast. He said he hadn't time to eat, but she said she'd left him to sleep on and now he wasn't going anywhere until he'd had a good breakfast. He argued no further.

He arrived at the station at a quarter to nine and went up to his room. He was checking through the mail when Detective-Constable Burrows came into the room. ' 'Morning, sir. Detective-Superintendent Akers has been asking for you.'

'Any particular reason?'

'I'm not certain. He seemed a bit impatient.'

Clayton wondered what the stolid Burrows meant by 'a bit impatient'. 'Where's he now?'

'He was around a moment ago, sir. He did keep asking if all the arrangements had been made for a press conference at ten o'clock sharp.'

'Hell!' muttered Clayton. 'Look, Abe, go and telephone the local papers and tell 'em to come along at ten, but warn 'em it's nothing fresh. And then see if you can find Sergeant Morris and send him along here.'

Burrows left. Burrows, thought Clayton, was stolid, unimaginative, and not particularly bright, but when you really considered the matter you realized how much any police force depended on men like him: they were the ones who would carry out the routine investigations that went on and on and they would not, because of their lack of imagintion, become inefficient through too much impatience at work which seemingly offered no return.

Morris came into the room. ' 'Morning, sir,' he said.

Clayton scrumpled up the last of the circular letters and threw it into the waste-paper basket. 'What happened with your interview?'

Morris smirked. 'As a matter of fact, sir, I've already reported to Mr Akers.'

'Then now you can have the added pleasure of reporting a second time, to me.'

Morris's expression became slightly sullen. 'I went to Trighton and saw the girl. She's a real snappy tart. It's a long time since I saw anyone . . . quite so openly sexy.'

She'd certainly made an impression, thought Clayton.

'She's known old Knott for about nine months. She works in a flower shop and he came in to buy some flowers, saw her, and from that moment on chased her as hard as he could go. She says he went really soft on her.'

'What d'you reckon her feelings were?'

E

Morris smoothed down his already smooth black hair with the palm of his hand. 'I'd say she found him a dirty old man who she was playing for all she could get.'

'In other words, just taking him for a ride?'

'Must have been, mustn't she? She'd want someone younger and more vigorous.'

'Like you?'

Morris failed to accept the question as a sarcastic one. 'That's right,' he said complacently. 'By the way, sir, whilst I was there a boy-friend of hers turned up. He was in his mid-twenties and really sharp. When she told him who I was, he looked mean—the way an ex-con always looks mean when he meets the law.'

'Check through the mug shots and see if you can find him.'

'I was going to.'

Of course, thought Clayton! 'Does she know about the forty thousand quid life insurance?'

'I threw out some hints, but she didn't bite. Only thing is, I gained the impression that she knows a lot more than she's letting on to.'

'It wasn't more than an impression?'

Morris shook his head. 'No.'

'Right. I want you now to . . .'

'Mr Akers has told me to get on to Louthy Products head office for help in tracing Alexander's sister and also to have a word with the Atherstone police.'

'You'd better do that, then, hadn't you?'

Morris turned and crossed to the door. He spoke as he opened it. 'Mr Akers is quite a live-wire, isn't he?' There was open admiration in his voice.

'I suppose he is. Which means he'd better not get mixed up or he'll blow a fuse.'

Morris looked at Clayton in a pitying way, then left. Clayton settled back in the chair. Morris was many things, but he wasn't a fool. If he gained the impression that Hazel

Clews knew something about the life insurance, that was a likely possibility.

He looked at his watch and saw the time was half-past nine. If he was to escape the press conference, he'd better get out of the station smartly.

He went down and out to the courtyard. On the far side of this were five lock-up garages, for the Panda and patrol cars which worked from the station, and a search bay for vehicles.

The half-ton van that had been found at Knott Farm was in the search bay. A uniformed constable, in overalls, was in the pit, using a trailing light to check underneath the car, and DC Pritchard was searching the interior.

Clayton spoke to Pritchard. 'Anything turned up?'

'Not really, sir,' boomed Pritchard. 'Just a letter that was under the front seat. There's nothing of interest in it.'

Clayton read the letter. It was signed Alice and was in the same handwriting as the two letters found in Alexander's room. There was no address, but the postmark was Atherstone and the date the first of August. He read the spidery writing. Joe had died after his accident and a month in hospital and his funeral had been the biggest seen for years: Joe's wife was having a terrible time with the kids. Angela Puttock had run off with a salesman. Old Mrs Fortes had gone barmy and there was some scandal the family had somehow managed to hush up. He handed the letter back. 'Has Dabs been over the car?'

'Yes, sir.'

'No luck?'

'No. There just weren't any prints.'

'D'you mean Dabs didn't find a single one?'

'That's right.' Pritchard jerked a large thumb in the direction of the paper sacks in the back of the van. 'The cow cake in them smells good enough to eat.'

Clayton made no answer and walked slowly over to his car. It seemed odd that there should be no finger-prints at all on the van. Admittedly the surfaces inside any vehicle smooth enough and large enough to take prints were far fewer than might be imagined, yet to drive a van round the countryside without leaving a single print . . . Would anyone in this heat wear gloves?

A uniformed constable came up to the car. 'Excuse me, sir.'

Clayton recognized him as one of the PCs who had been sent out to Endley Cross to make general enquiries. 'Yes?'

'I was asking around the village, sir, and spoke to the landlord of the pub out there—it's his wife what runs the place during the day. He said he saw a van going up the farm drive at about a quarter past two.'

'How sure is he of the time?'

'Near enough exact, sir. He was back in the pub at twenty past for certain.'

'Can he tell us anything about the van?'

'It was a green one, from Louthy Products. He's got a few chickens and buys their grub from that firm, so that's why he noticed.'

'Could he see the driver?'

'No, sir.'

Clayton thanked the PC, who left. One time was now established—Alexander had driven up to the farm at two-fifteen.

Clayton drove out of the courtyard on to the road. There was considerable traffic, especially by the entrance to the diesel factory, and it was not until he was beyond the town that he was able to relax. He loved the countryside and all that went on in it, having a sympathy with the slower pace of living, a quiet acceptance of a life that was so largely ruled by the most arbitrary of all things, the English weather. In other circumstances, he would have liked to have been a farmer. Perhaps, when he retired, he and Margery could somehow find enough money to buy a small place in the country . . . He grinned. Nothing so effectively cured an ambition, so the cynics said, as attaining it. As a towns-man—he'd always lived in towns—he was inclined to think of the countryside as perpetually bathed in warm sun-shine, the only sounds the chirping of birds and the droning of insects : what about mud a foot deep, electricity cuts, roads blocked by snow, doctors who wouldn't attend a patient who lived several miles from the surgery?

He reached Endley Cross and saw two cars parked out-side the pub : was the landlord breaking the laws and open-ing a bit early? He didn't know and didn't care. He con-tinued over the cross-roads and came to the beginning of the woods on the left and the first of the fields belonging to Knott Farm on the right, a field thick with docks and thistles. How could Knott have allowed the place to fall into such disrepair? A man had to be completely insensible to do that, unable to appreciate that he was in honour bound to pass on the inheritance he had received. He passed the farmhouse, then on the left the ornamental gates across the drive up to the hidden derelict house, and continued down the short hill to Browland's cottage.

He stood in the garden and carefully admired the serried rows of vegetables. When he turned back towards the cot-tage, he saw the edge of the curtains of the downstairs room move. He knocked and Meg opened the door. She stared up at him and her small, peaked face held both challenge and fear.

'I'm sorry to bother you again,' he said in friendly tones. 'I've just had a look at your garden—I've never seen such vegetables.'

Shyly, she said that her husband often won prizes at the local village flower-show and when he said he wasn't sur-prised and had they thought of entering larger shows, she became quite talkative. After a while, she asked him if he'd like a cup of tea and he replied that nothing would be more welcome. They went inside.

His tea was served in a chipped mug, but she was now

sufficiently at ease not to bother to apologise. He offered her a cigarette, but she refused. 'By the way,' he asked, 'does your husband work up at the farm all morning?'

''E don't, because 'e ain't paid for it,' she answered. 'What's more, there's someone turned up there what says 'e's the new owner. Tom says 'e's good at givin' orders. We don't know what's going to 'appen to us.' A look of deep worry crossed her face.

'Mr Hulton will have to have help—you can't run a dairy farm that size on your own.'

'It ain't everyone what'll employ Tom,' she said candidly.

'But I hear he's a first-class milker.'

'He's that all right—and he gets on well with animals.'

'He'll be OK. If Tom's not at the farm, I suppose he's here?'

'Yes, 'e is . . .' She suddenly stared at him with renewed fear.

'Mrs Browland, I promise you I'm not going to harm him. I just want a word with him.'

''E's . . . 'e's afraid of the police, always 'as been.' Hastily, she added: 'Not that 'e's any cause to be.'

'Tell him that he's absolutely no cause to be afraid of me.'

She studied his face and was relieved by what she saw. She left and he heard her climb uncarpeted stairs. A murmur of voices came from above and after a while she returned with Browland. He remained close to her and was so nervous that he couldn't keep still, but kept fidgeting with his nose. He was wearing the same clothes as he had been the night before.

'Those are some wonderful marrows you've got outside,' said Clayton. 'I don't think I've ever seen their equal.'

In next to no time, Browland was chatting happily about his garden and when Clayton eventually brought the subject round to the murders, he seemed quite unafraid.

'I came back here because I thought you might remember something more,' said Clayton. 'You know how things go—one day you clean forget something, the next day it's clear in your mind. I'll tell you one of our big problems—what could have started the fire? Obviously once it was going, the diesel oil and paraffin helped it along a lot, but what started it?'

Browland left his wife's side and sat down. His brow furrowed as he thought hard. 'Maybe it were the 'lectricity,' he finally said.

'Why might it have been that?'

'It were in a terrible state. The man what came to look at it said it needed new wiring. Mr Knott said as 'e couldn't afford it.'

'D'you know where the wiring was so bad?'

'The 'lectricity man said it was real dangerous in the store-room.'

'That's the place where the fire was?'

'That's right.'

'D'you know who it was came and inspected the wiring?'

'It were Mike, from the village.'

'Who's he?'

'Mike Langham,' said Meg. ''E lives at Netsway Cottages, does a lot of work for people.'

Clayton noted down the name and address. When he looked up, he smiled at Browland. 'Now is there anything else, anything at all that might help?'

Browland shook his head. He began to fiddle with his nose once more and carefully did not look at Clayton.

'You didn't by chance see or hear anything early on Monday afternoon?'

Browland shook his head vigorously.

Meg hurriedly asked Clayton if he would like some more tea and he said he would. She refilled his mug, then went and stood by the chair in which Browland sat.

As Clayton stirred his tea, he said: 'There was a lovely smell of cooking here last night.'

Meg reached across with her hand and gripped her husband.

'If it weren't out of season, I'd have guessed it was pheasant.' He sipped his tea.

Browland's expression was one of terrified panic.

Clayton put the mug down on his knees. 'I'll tell you something. As far as I'm concerned, I don't care whether it was pheasant or chicken. All I'm interested in is hearing about Monday afternoon.'

Meg spoke in little more than a whisper. 'You . . . you ain't going to 'urt 'im, Mister?'

'I've already promised you I'll do nothing to hurt him.'

''E only . . . only did it 'cause it was our wedding anniversary and we couldn't afford nothing special.'

'Then that's all forgotten.' He spoke directly to Browland. 'Just what happened on Monday afternoon?'

Speaking jerkily, looking at his wife all the time, frequently fiddling with his nose, Browland told him how he'd left the house to go 'looking' in Parson's Wood.

Clayton listened in silence to the end, then said: 'You left the house at ten past two, walked through the woods, and heard this shot, checked on the time and it was five minutes past three? How correct's your watch?'

'It ain't never wrong,' Browland answered proudly.

'It don't never lose more'n a minute a day,' Meg said. 'It was dead right for the news on the telly last night.'

'Good. Now just think very carefully, then tell me how certain you are that the shot was on the farm or woods and from the direction of the buildings?'

Browland's face screwed up. 'The wind was from over there. That shot didn't come from nowhere else.'

It was very difficult to identify the direction of a shot, especially in woods, Clayton thought. 'Have you any idea what sort of gun it was?'

'It weren't a two-two, nor likely was it a four-ten.

Could've been two shots going off very close together, like. 'Ad a strange echo to it.'

'If I arrange to have a gun fired in the food store, could you go into the woods and see if the noise is the same?'

Browland grinned, as if the idea of being asked by the police to trespass was a wonderful one.

'Tell me about Knott, will you? Was he very difficult to work for?'

Browland was puzzled by the question and it had to be explained in simpler terms before he understood. ''E 'ad a temper and used to shout a lot and 'e didn't know much.'

'Did he ever do the milking?'

'Not 'im. Couldn't abide muck.'

'So what did he do? Work in the fields all day?'

'Like as not, 'e wouldn't do nothing. Used to go off a lot.'

'You mean, he left the farm?'

Browland nodded. 'That's right.'

'All day?'

'That's right.'

'Had he always done this sort of thing?'

'I don't rightly know, seeing as I ain't worked there afore the middle of last year. 'E was around the farm until just before Christmas, but 'e weren't around much after that.'

'Did he ever talk about making hay or silage for this year?'

'Never said nothing.'

'Have you any idea why he bought so much cow cake and stored it in the interior Dutch barn?'

Browland shook his head.

Clayton stood up. 'I'll be moving. Thanks very much for the talk and the tea.'

Meg spoke hesitatingly. 'You promised 'e wouldn't get into no trouble. But what if 'e 'as to say 'e was in them woods . . .?'

'There's no reason on earth why he shouldn't go for a walk in the woods to enjoy the peace.' Clayton winked.

Browland laughed, a strange, neighing, grunting sound.

Clayton left. He drove to the end of the road and turned right at the T-junction, continuing two hundred yards to the cross-roads around which the village of Cregiton was set. To the south, the land fell away and the sea was visible, six miles away. Netsway Cottages were a row of six semi-detached council houses which were to the left of the wooden school house and the village hut: on the other side of the road was the village pub.

Mrs Langham said her husband was out at work a couple of miles away and she gave him the address. He thanked her, then drove along the winding lanes, past acres of mixed woodland that had not yet been massacred by the Forestry Commission and was still a mélange of oak, ash, birch, hazel, hornbeam, bramble and bracken, and he reached the address, a small, pimply farmhouse. To the left were large and graceless concrete and asbestos buildings in which were calves being reared for veal. Langham was working in the first of these buildings. He said he'd been called to Knott Farm in July to inspect the wiring in the wing nearest the road. He'd never seen wiring like it: it was perished from one end to the other. Why the whole place hadn't gone up in smoke a couple of years before was a mystery: the slightest disturbance to the wires would creat a short. If anyone from the Electricity Board had seen it, the electricity would have been cut off until every last inch of wiring had been renewed. Yet Knott had said he couldn't afford to do anything.

Clayton arrived back at the police station at half-past eleven. When he entered his room, he found another desk had been installed and on this were two typewriters, two telephones, and a number of folders. Detective-Sergeant Bodmin sat to the side of the desk, typing.

'Make yourself at home, won't you?' said Clayton.

'Sorry, sir, but Mr Akers said we were to work in here.'

'Perhaps it would be better if I moved out?'

Bodmin went on typing.

The door slammed open and Akers hurried in. 'So you've finally managed to arrive, Inspector?'

'Did you want me, sir?'

'Want you? Of course I goddamn wanted you. Did I not order a press conference for ten o'clock this morning?'

'Yes, sir.'

'Why didn't you attend it?'

'I gathered you'd be conducting it, sir, so I thought I could get on with some work.'

'And just what work did you get on with?' demanded Akers.

'Finding out the time of the murder, sir.'

Clayton met the divisional superintendent in the corridor. 'How are things, Jim?' asked the superintendent.

'I suppose they could just be worse, sir.'

The superintendent smiled.

'Were you at the press conference by any chance?' asked Clayton.

'No, I wasn't.'

'Then I suppose you've no idea whether any London reporters turned up?'

'I did hear that it was only a couple of the local ones again.'

'Aren't we a dozy lot of country bumpkins?' It was Clayton's turn to smile.

CHAPTER VIII

To THE NORTH-WEST of Gertfinden was an area which in the Edwardian era had been where the wealthy settled: large houses had been built, each in an extensive garden. In the course of time, most of the original labour-demanding houses had either been turned into flats or had been demolished, to make way for blocks of modern four- and five-storey flats.

Elizabeth Corrins's house, in Challock Road, was one of the few Edwardian houses which had survived. It was obvious that either the architect or the first owner had been an impractical romantic, for the house possessed a columned porch, a cupola, and at one end a square tower with crenellated roof-line. The result was both architecturally ugly and—in the bright sunshine which added a feeling of lightness—visually appealing in a cheerfully dotty manner.

Clayton parked his car behind the rusting Bentley of Mrs Knott. He walked across the gravel to the front porch, which was twelve feet high and wouldn't have disgraced a mansion. He knocked on the iron-studded, wooden door and waited. On the front lawn, a man was mowing the grass.

Miss Corrins opened the front door. As soon as she saw him, the expression on her square, heavy face hardened. 'Well?'

'May I have a word with Mrs Knott?'

Miss Corrins hesitated, as if about to deny her friend was there, then she looked past him and saw the Bentley. 'Come in,' she said ungraciously.

He stepped into the hall. There was a magnificent Persian carpet on the floor, while above it hung three framed coloured prints which surely must have come from Xmas cards: an early settle with a most beautiful patina stood next to a leprous-looking elephant's leg in which were half-a-dozen cheap souvenir walking-sticks. Money and no taste, he thought: still, that was surely preferable to a state of taste and no money.

The large sitting-room ran the length of the house and in this too was the same combination of rich, beautiful furniture and furnishings and cheap, tasteless ones. Mrs Knott sat in a tooled leather arm-chair, while by her side was a stained, scratched, clumsy wooden table.

'I'm very sorry to have to come and trouble you again,' he said to Mrs Knott.

'She's very, very upset,' snapped Miss Corrins.

'Of course.'

Miss Corrins stared angrily at him, then went across and sat on the arm of Mrs Knott's chair, overflowing it and looking most precarious. She rested her hand on the other woman's shoulder and quite suddenly Clayton realized what it was about Miss Corrins he so disliked. He wondered how it could ever have taken him so long to understand.

No one had asked him to sit down, but he was hot and tired and he sat. 'Mrs Knott, do you happen to know what system of winter feeding your husband was intending to use this year?'

She looked surprised, but said nothing, merely shaking her head.

'Did you in fact have much to do with the farm—did you help with the accounts, for instance?'

'No.'

'Then you wouldn't be able to tell me anything about the farm's use of fertilizer?'

'No.' She suddenly looked up and her mouth twisted. 'Whatever he did it wasn't right. When we started it was all going to be so wonderful and then . . .'

Miss Corrins interrupted her. 'His trouble was, he was too stupid : thought he knew everything, but didn't know anything.'

'It was all going to be so wonderful,' said Mrs Knott, for the second time. She blinked rapidly. 'We were the Knotts of Knott Farm. Daniel's ancestors had owned the estate for centuries. He was Lord of the Manor. Did you know that?'

'Was he really?' said Clayton.

She began to speak more rapidly, not really to them but to herself. 'Daniel's grandfather refused a title. There used to be family portraits of all the Knotts in the sitting-room of the big house : Daniel told me about them. You could see the family all the way back to the Civil War : there aren't many families can do that. When we first lived on the farm, Daniel was invited to lots of shoots and the hunt met in the drive. The MFH suggested I learned to ride. But it didn't last. They were all so snobby. It wasn't my fault I wasn't born into their kind of family : why were they so horrible to me? Some of them couldn't take their ancestors back two generations.'

Clayton felt uncomfortably disturbed at witnessing such intense grief over something he had always considered totally irrelevant.

'They first of all stopped inviting us back,' she said dully, 'then made weak excuses when we asked them to us. Daniel was rude to some of them—he always had such a hasty temper . . .'

He interrupted her recital of misery. 'Mrs Knott, can you confirm that the estate is entailed through to your nephew?'

Tears spilled down her cheeks. 'It's not fair. Why should it go to Paul and leave me with almost nothing? What am I going to live on? What am I going to do?'

'Don't worry, Phyllis,' said Miss Corrins. She moved her hand along the other's shoulder until she could stroke her neck. 'You'll be all right with me.'

'Paul shouldn't have it. He's so crude. He's no right to be in that position—he's nothing but a farm labourer.'

'Did you see much of Paul Hulton?' he asked.

'He was always turning up and telling Daniel that everything he did was wrong. What right had Paul to do that?'

'Did he seem to get worked up about the state of the farm?'

'Sometimes he was so rude. He said that in five years Daniel had ruined a good farm and made it almost dere- lict. He told me that if Daniel had the farm for another two years it would be completely derelict and when he inherited it it wouldn't be worth a farthing.' Mrs Knott spoke loudly.

'Daniel was a wonderful farmer and if only he'd had a little more time . . .'

'He'd have turned the place into a desert,' snapped Miss Corrins.

Mrs Knott turned and faced her. 'But Liz, you know that's not very kind. He was a very good farmer and it was only . . .'

'Stuff and nonsense. He knew nothing. He was the stupidest, most pig-headed man I've ever met.'

De mortuis nil nisi bonum, thought Clayton, recalling the only Latin he had ever known. 'Mrs Knott, what was your husband finally intending to do about the wiring in the store-room at the farm?'

'Wiring?' she said vaguely.

'Didn't you know an electrician checked it in July and said it was in a critically dangerous state?'

She shook her head.

'Mrs Knott, did your husband have any life insurance?'

'I don't know,' she said dully.

'Then you weren't aware that he took out a policy for forty thousand pounds?'

Her surprise was immediate. 'He . . . did what?'

'In March of this year, he took out a life insurance for forty thousand pounds.'

'But . . . Are you sure?'

'I've spoken to the insurance company.'

'Then . . . then there's all that money for me?'

'I'm afraid you're not the beneficiary. A Miss Hazel Clews was named in the policy.'

She closed her eyes and her mouth twisted into lines of deep and bitter hatred.

'I'm sorry to have to ask you this,' he said, 'but did you know your husband was acquainted with a young lady of that name?'

She shook her head, still with closed eyes.

'She lives at Trighton-on-Sea.'

She said nothing.

'He saw quite a lot of her.'

She opened her eyes. 'That's a lie,' she shouted, her voice shrill. 'He wouldn't have done anything like that: he was a Knott. D'you hear, it's a lie.'

'Miss Clews admits to the friendship.'

'She just wants to make out she knew him because of who he was.'

'Don't you think he must have known her, since he named her the beneficiary of his life insurance?'

'It's all a lie.'

She'd been tormented by her knowledge of what was going on, he thought.

'He was fool enough to get trapped by any young bitch,' said Miss Corrins maliciously.

Clayton stood up. 'I won't worry you very much longer, but there's just one last thing. Will you tell me where you were on Monday afternoon at three?'

Mrs Knott didn't answer.

He put the question to her again.

'I was here,' she muttered.

'Can anyone substantiate that?'

'She was here all day,' snapped Miss Corrins. 'Now if you've finished, clear out of my house.'

With the greatest of pleasure, he thought.

Clayton hurried up the stairs in the police station and when he reached the top he was perspiring so freely that he stopped and mopped his face with a handkerchief. He must be getting old—one flight of stairs and he was reduced to a grease spot. Margery said he ate too much—but then she was such a rattling good cook.

He crossed the landing and went into his room. Bodmin was sitting at the second desk and Akers was pacing the floor. 'Well?' demanded Akers.

'Mrs Knott obviously knew about the girl, but won't

admit it,' said Clayton. He went round his desk and sat down. He longed to take off his coat, loosen his tie, and undo the top shirt button, but felt certain that Akers, who looked smoothly cool, would be enraged by such slovenliness.

'Has she any alibi?' asked Akers.

'She says she was at Challock Road all day and the old bitch confirms that.'

'To whom are you referring?' asked Akers coldly.

'Miss Corrins,' replied Clayton, and sighed.

Akers paced across to the window, turned smartly, paced back to the second desk, turned smartly, paced back to the centre of the room and there stopped. 'Where are your time correlation, statement time-check, and statement and information cross-check charts, Inspector?'

Clayton mopped his forehead yet again. 'I haven't drawn any up, sir.'

'Why not?'

'As a matter of fact, I've always managed without such things.'

'I suppose you know what I'm talking about?'

'Yes, sir.'

'Then I suggest you draw up such charts. This is not the age of the horse and buggy.'

'No, sir.'

Akers crossed to the small mirror on the wall and checked that his tie was neatly tied. 'Have you been on the phone to Louthy's?'

'Not yet, sir,' replied Clayton.

Akers turned away from the mirror. 'Time in the country does not seem to be a precious commodity.' He walked out of the room.

Detective-Sergeant Bodmin put some papers into one of the folders. He then placed the folder carefully and exactly on top of the others.

'You must lead a very busy life,' said Clayton.

F

'It's different, sir,' replied Bodmin. He left.

Clayton used the internal telephone to speak to Morris. 'George, the superintendent has made a suggestion that we draw up time correlation charts and that sort of thing. How does that strike you as an idea?'

'A jolly good one, sir : as you know, I've always said we should go for the modern methods of crime detection.'

'Excellent. Draw them up.' He replaced the receiver.

He leaned back in his chair and lit a cigarette. What was it like to be Mrs Knott, tortured by problems that any reasonable person would laugh at? What agonies had she suffered because people had never accepted her as one of the true Knotts? It was so easy to call her a fool and dismiss all her heartaches as stupidity, but that was to be objective, and when you were dealing with people's emotions you had to be entirely subjective. It didn't matter if anyone else considered Mrs Knott a fool to think as she did—that's how she thought. To learn that her husband had taken up with a chit of a girl must have been gall and wormwood to her.

He slid down his tie and undid the top button of his shirt. Jersey must be heaven in such weather . . . He told himself this wasn't the way to make his fortune and sat upright, picked up the telephone receiver, and asked the switchboard operator to get him Louthy's head office. When the connection was made, he spoke to the manager.

'We've been checking as your man asked us to,' said the manager, 'but I'm sorry, we don't seem to be able to tell you much. We advertised two vacancies for salesmen working on a commission basis, one in the south-east, one in Wales, and Alexander applied for the south-east. In his letter of application, he said he'd been a salesman for a food products firm in the Midlands and knew a little about farming because his father had been a farmer. We had him along for an interview, liked the look of him, and took him on.'

'Did you ask for references?'

'He gave us some from his previous employers.'

'Did you follow them up?'

'Not really, no. You know what it is today—references don't really mean all that much in the normal course of things, but one still demands 'em. A lot of employers will give first-class ones just to get rid of a bloke. In any case, Alexander said his old firm had been taken over and the personnel had either left or been shifted up to Yorkshire. As a matter of fact, when it comes to taking on a new bloke, we rely almost wholly on the interview. He had a reasonable personality and knew something about farming.'

'How did he make out on the job?'

'He put the sales of our products up almost ten per cent, except for one area.'

'So you were satisfied with him?'

'We'd no cause to be otherwise. Not until you told us about the fertilizer business, that is.'

'And what's the result of your inquiries into that?'

'I'm afraid it does seem there may have been a swindle going on. All subsidy application forms are stamped by us with the firm's name stamp and are then signed by either Mr Hatchard or Mr Nathen. I've inquired about fertilizer orders Alexander handled and in not one case were the subsidy forms signed by anyone else.'

'What about the amounts that were actually delivered to East, Wright, and Woolcott?'

'Hang on a sec and I'll find the list . . . Here we are. Five tons of compound to East, four of high N to Wright, five tons of nitro chalk to Woolcott.'

'Have you supplied fertilizer to any of these farmers before?'

'Only to East. He had five tons of high N in May.'

'Good, I've got that . . . Had any luck in tracing Alexander's relatives?'

'I'm sorry, but all I can do for you there is give you the notes I made at the interview. Alexander came south from

Atherstone after his wife died because he didn't want to stay in the area and also because his firm had been taken over. He told us he'd stay on at his digs in Relstone if given the job. That's the lot, really.'

'Many thanks.'

'I say, d'you think our firm's name is going to come out in all this because of the fertilizer subsidy?'

'I don't really see how it can be avoided,' replied Clayton.

'What a hell of a mess,' said the manager gloomily.

CHAPTER IX

WHEN CLAYTON arrived home, Margery was weeding one of the rose-beds in the back garden. 'You shouldn't be doing that in this heat,' he protested.

She sat back on the lawn. 'If I don't do it now, the bind-weed will strangle the roses.'

'I told you I'd cope when I had the time.'

'I can't quite remember whether that was back in late May or early June.'

He grinned. 'You're a liar.'

'I am not. Now tell me what you're doing home at such a respectable hour as six in the evening? Has that revolting superintendent calmed down?'

'Far from it. That odious illegitimate has ordered me out to Torrinden to see a farmer. I just thought I'd call in for a cuppa on the way.'

'But this isn't on the way from the police station to Tor-rinden.'

'I know that, love, but the superintendent doesn't.'

They went into the house and she made tea and offered him some newly made scones. He ate five, very liberally buttered, and only refused a sixth with reluctance.

The farm in Torrinden was set back from the road, along

a rough track. The farmhouse was moderately sized and remarkable for two tall, round, period chimneys with spiralled brick-work. East was large, heavily built, red-faced, and he had the bonhomie of a man who set out to be the life and soul of every party he went to. He offered Clayton a beer and poured out two pints into pewter tankards, saying as he did so that half-pints were for boys and invalids. His cheerfulness continued until Clayton mentioned fertilizers.

'Fertilizers?' he said.

'That's right. How much did you order?'

East drank heavily. He wiped his mouth with the back of his hand. 'I . . . I ordered ten tons.'

'Has it all been delivered?'

'Aye. And it's out on the grass.'

'Using that much at this time of the year must mean you're hoping for a third cut?'

East again drank heavily. 'It's good ground round here. Grass keeps growing and the animals keep on eating it.'

'But if you've put on compound, you surely can't graze the grass?'

'Some people say you have to worry about hypermag if you do, but it's too late in the year for that and anyway most experts don't know what in the hell they're talking about.' He laughed loudly. 'Like I've always said, Inspector, them as can farm do, them as can't become agricultural experts.'

'I think you also had some high nitrogen in May?'

'That's right. And that lot went out on to the paddocks. The bloke who invented paddock grazing knew a thing or two. Not that it makes your fortune, mind, or even a reasonable return on capital. The bloody government takes care of that. They allow us just enough income to make certain we don't despair completely and hang ourselves or sell up and take the capital abroad.'

'How much nitrogen did you have in May?'

'By the end of a season, I reckon to use three hundred units an acre . . .'

'How many tons of nitrogen were delivered in May?'

East drank, looked quickly at the DI, then away. 'You didn't say exactly why you'd come here.'

'That's right, I didn't.'

'But it's something to do with fertilizers?'

'I'm investigating the death of Daniel Knott.'

East immediately became very much more cheerful. 'The bloke who was burned to death and had been shot? I read about him in the papers. Now there's a rum do . . .'

'Mr East, how many tons of nitrogen were delivered here in May?'

East drained his tankard. 'I don't see what all that's got to do with Knott,' he said resentfully.

'You will.'

East crossed to the table on which were several bottles of beer and opened one. The beer sprayed out. He fumbled badly in getting the mug under the bottle and beer hit the wall to the right of the large open fireplace and trickled down it.

'You know,' said Clayton quietly, 'you'll have to tell me in the end.'

East filled his tankard with the beer left in the bottle. 'It was ten tons. When you put on a couple of hundredweight after . . .'

'And were you paid the subsidy on ten tons?'

'That . . . that's right,' he said reluctantly.

'And you will expect to be paid the subsidy on the ten tons of compound fertilizer you ordered and received recently?'

'Yes.'

'Yet Louthy Products in each case only supplied you with five tons of fertilizer and that's how they marked the two fertilizer subsidy application forms.'

East sat down. He drank the beer in vast swallows and then gripped the tankard with both hands.

'How long has the racket been going on?' asked Clayton.

East's face became a picture of abject misery. 'It's not my fault—it's the government's.'

'I suppose that's one way of excusing oneself!'

'I swear I wouldn't have done anything like it if the government had ever given a damn about farmers. Prices go on rising and rising, yet what we get for the milk remains the same. I'm not like some lucky bastards, I don't own this farm—I'm a tenant. So what can I do? My income's gone down by a third in two years, yet I can't sell up and get a large capital sum. When the bloke came along selling stuff and he suggested I get a bit of extra money from the government, well . . . It wasn't stealing, d'you understand?'

'What would you call it, then?'

'I was getting in a bit of the money the bloody government owed me, but wouldn't give me.'

Clayton made no comment.

'What's going to happen?' muttered East.

'I can't say.'

'Do you . . . Does this have to go to court?'

'I shall report the facts. The action that's taken is decided by other people.'

'Suppose . . . suppose I paid you all the money . . .'

'I don't know whether you're offering to bribe me,' said Clayton, and his voice was suddenly harsh, 'but I strongly advise against the attempt.'

East lifted up the tankard and tried to drink. He was surprised to find it empty. He looked appealingly at the DI, then hurriedly away.

'How exactly did you get caught up in this?' asked Clayton.

Haltingly, in a low voice that was in complete contrast to his earlier bombastic one, East said: 'The salesman from Louthy's came to try to get me to buy from them. He promised top discount and two months to pay instead of the usual one. I had some cake off him. Next time, he asked about fertilizers and said they were going up in price soon and if I wanted some I should order quick. I had a good moan about the rising prices and he said there was a way of cutting costs and . . . and then . . .'

'You joined in the fraud. How did you share the extra money?'

'Fifty-fifty.' His misery increased. 'It didn't come to very much. If I'd only known . . .' He stopped.

That, thought Clayton, was the constant cry of the amateur criminal. 'If I'd only known.'

For supper, Margery had bought a broiler and then cooked it with such care and a cunning selection of herbs that instead of being tasteless it was delicious. Clayton had two helpings and would have had a third had the carcass not, by then, been picked clean. 'You spoil me,' he said contentedly, as he stacked the dirty plates.

'I know.'

He stood up and carried the plates across the kitchen to the sink. 'What's for afters?'

'Chocolate mousse and some of that special double cream I buy from the little shop round the corner.'

The telephone rang. 'Damn and blast!' he muttered.

'Don't you go, Jim,' she said. 'If it is for you I'll tell them you're still out at work. You've done more than enough for the day.'

He shook his head. 'I'd better handle it, love. It could be important.' He went into the hall. The call was from Detective-Superintendent Barry. 'How are things going, Jim?'

'We're gradually getting the picture, sir.'

'Good, good. Mr Akers is a very efficient officer.'

'So he tells me.'

'It's a good job we called him in. This is a big case, isn't it, Jim?'

'It is indeed.'

'So much better to have called him in. Well, I'm glad everything's going well. Good night.'

Clayton returned to the kitchen. 'I'm glad one bloke's happy,' he said.

CHAPTER X

THE REPORT from the forensic scientist arrived Thursday morning. He could add no new facts in respect of Knott's body, but had found traces of Barbital-Veronal in Alexander's body. He confirmed that Alexander had eaten a meal about three hours previous to death and part of that meal had consisted of meat, dumplings, and greens. The pieces of metal found among the debris of the burned-out section of the farm buildings were mainly of a ferrous nature, but there were two small lumps of brass: in no case was it possible to say what articles these had been before the fire.

Clayton met Akers and Bodmin in the courtyard of the station as he was on his way out and they were on their way in. 'The report from the lab is in my room, sir,' said Clayton.

Akers ordered him back upstairs. They went up to his room and he handed over the report. After reading through it, Akers looked up. 'Have you checked what Barbital-Veronal is exactly?' he asked.

'Yes, sir.'

Akers looked faintly surprised. He was wearing a light-weight grey suit, a white striped shirt with semi-stiff collar, and what appeared to be an old school tie. His black hair was smoothly in place, his face was untroubled by sweat. He looked like an up-and-thrusting executive, about to be voted on to the board.

'It's a long-acting barbiturate,' said Clayton. 'Takes an hour or so to work and traces remain in the body for twenty-four hours if the dose is strong enough.'

'He obviously took some the previous night. Extraordinary how many people these days are so dependent on drugs.'

'You know,' said Clayton, 'that meal just doesn't make sense. Monday was a boiling hot day and to tuck into a really hot, heavy meal like that . . .'

'There are always odd facts to any case, Inspector, and it's one of the investigator's tasks to ignore those which obviously have no bearing on the case. What was the result of your interview with East?'

'The report is there on your desk, sir. There was a subsidy fiddle going on.'

'What was the full extent of it?'

Clayton sighed. 'It hasn't been possible to determine that figure yet, sir.'

'Don't you think it's rather an important one? And we'd also better determine what kind of alibi the nephew and Miss Clews have for the time of death.'

'Yes, sir.'

'You told me you were going to fire a gun in the farm building and have that half-wit in the woods see if he thought the noise was the same—has that been done?'

'DC Burrows borrowed Mr Knott's gun from Mrs Knott and fired it in the food store, first one barrel then the two together. Browland was in the woods and he says the two barrels together produced the same kind of noise and the direction was right.'

'I suppose that's the best we'll be able to do.' Akers went behind his desk and sat down. Detective-Sergeant Bodmin remained standing. After a while Akers said challengingly to Clayton: 'Is there anything more?'

'I'm not really certain. It's just that I've a feeling . . .' He tailed off into silence.

'A feeling? What's that supposed to mean?'

'A feeling,' said Clayton doggedly, 'that we're not really getting to grips with the case.'

Akers looked annoyed.

'I don't think we're at the heart of it, if you know what I mean?'

'No, I don't.'

'Surely, sir, you sometimes get an instinct about a case?'

'I have learned to deal in facts.'

'I've always found a case has a rhythm to it and when that rhythm seems to break up . . .'

'Inspector, what on earth are you talking about?'

'I'm afraid it's not readily explainable.' Clayton rubbed his chin and wondered how in the hell he had been such a fool as to start this conversation. 'It's just that . . . Well, take the cake.'

'What cake?'

'The cattle cake in the interior Dutch barn. There are several tons there—why?'

Akers leaned back in his chair. 'You still aren't prepared to accept the fact that the cattle food might actually have been for the cattle to eat?'

'Those cows are being fed on a very low-cost ration and as it's August most of their needs are still being met by the grass—it's only necessary to feed for the last couple of gallons, or so, and that's being done with the crushed barley. That cake costs something over thirty quid a ton and so there's several hundred quid lying about in the barn. With the way the farm was doing, Knott just couldn't afford to wrap up that sort of money, merely to get discount for summer buying.'

'Then perhaps there's another swindle here?'

'How can there be? There's no subsidy on cattle cake.'

Akers shrugged his shoulders. 'You tell me the farm is run down and doing very badly so perhaps the man was a fool as well as incompetent.'

'Why isn't there any hay or silage for winter feed?'

'How the hell should I know why?'

'You've got to have some sort of bulk feed for the winter. He couldn't have afforded a ration of barley straw and an additive.'

'Are we not agreed that he was incompetent?'

'But having no hay or silage is criminal folly.'

'Criminal?'

'Just a manner of speech, sir.'

Akers looked bored.

'Then there's the medical evidence. D'you remember the pathologist's report about the blow to Alexander's head which was quite enough to kill him, yet he'd gone on breathing?'

'He died because he suffocated.'

'What I mean is . . .'

'Does it matter, Inspector?'

'What about the van?'

'What about it?'

'When Dabs checked it, there weren't any finger-prints at all.'

Akers picked up a pencil and fiddled with it. 'On the face of things, that might be held a trifle odd. But Alexander may have looked after it with much greater pride than's usual and may very recently have cleaned the interior. By chance, on the drive to the farm, he may not have put his fingers on any surface that would take prints.'

'It . . . it doesn't seem really likely. And nothing explains the meal that Alexander had eaten.'

Akers dropped the pencil on to the desk. 'Inspector, as a specialist, I investigate a large number of murders, or suspected murders, all over the country. When were you last concerned with one?'

Clayton thought back. 'I suppose it was some time ago.'

'And were you then in charge of investigations?'

'No, sir.'

'Then I suggest you take careful note of something—in

any case you investigate, especially murder, it is a golden rule that ninety-nine times out of a hundred it is the obvious which is the truth.'

'But odd facts . . .'

'Are almost certainly completely extraneous. In basic terms, what have we here? Two men who have died in circumstances that point to their having killed each other in the course of a fraud. In dying, one fell against the very dangerous electric wires which shorted out and started a fire that was fed by paraffin and diesel oil. That, Inspector, is the obvious picture. Now I trust you don't believe I could have overlooked the alternative?'

'Of course not.'

'The alternative is that both deaths were engineered by someone who thereby benefited. Obviously it is only Knott's death that can benefit someone—so if he'd been murdered by a third party, it would have been when he was on his own : no murderer is going to kill two people when one's enough. Suppose we ignore that very elementary fact and go on to ask ourselves who has a motive for Knott's death? We get the names of his wife, the nephew, and the Clews woman. The wife has a corroborated alibi for the time of death and you are going to check the alibis of the other two this morning, aren't you?'

'Yes, sir.'

'Then if we discover each of the three has a good alibi, we know that although he or she may benefit from the death, none of them murdered Knott. D'you agree?'

'Yes, sir.'

'Thank God for that! Now go out and check the essential facts and stop worrying about cow cake and dumplings.'

Clayton left and went back to the courtyard, climbed into his car, and lit a cigarette. On the face of things, Akers was perfectly right—yet Clayton could not stop feeling certain the odd facts were somehow of significance. Yet was his certainty really pig-headedness? Was he being a fool? After all, Akers knew a hell of a lot more about murders than he did. Shouldn't he just shut up? A cynical detective-constable had once said, on his retirement, that he'd gained no promotion because he'd never learned to agree with all his superiors in all cases at all times. What was to be gained in this case—other than trouble—by continually angering Akers?

He started the car's engine. If Hulton and Hazel Clews, as well as Mrs Knott, had alibis, there really could be no room for further argument.

Paul Hulton was mole-draining a twenty-acre field when Clayton, coat off, tie undone, finally found him. He drew the mole through a patch of rushes, continued to the end of the field, stopped, and lifted the mole on the three-point linkage. He pulled out the control button and the engine shuddered to a stop.

Clayton studied him as he climbed down. He was a very strong man, so compactly built that some of his height was masked. His heavy features suggested a bitter, determined character, always fighting for what he wanted, not very likeable, but a man who never knew the meaning of defeat. 'Sorry to stop the good work,' said Clayton.

Hulton stretched. 'I'm not complaining at a break—so long as it's short.'

'You've a job on your hands with this place.'

'It'll be a bloody miracle if I can get things straight in five years, working fifteen hours a day.' He gestured violently. 'How the hell could anyone let a place get in this state? This clay doesn't make for good farming, but the place was reasonable when Reggie had it. Trouble was, Daniel thought he was going to be squire. Like every other bloody stupid gentleman farmer, he hired a manager as lazy as he was crooked. Then there was the shoot. Full-time keeper, big shooting parties, saddle of mutton and mulled wine on the table. And d'you know where the money for

all that came from? From this land. Ditches weren't kept
dug, hedges grew out, drains blocked up, the dung wasn't
put out, no basic slag was bought, he wouldn't use the
premium bulls from the AI because they cost more . . .'
Hulton kicked a large clod of earth with such violence that
it broke up and splattered the surrounding land.

'You can't have had much time for him, seeing all this
going on.'

'When I read in the papers he was likely dead, I called it
a miracle.'

'His death did someone some good, then?'

Hulton wiped the sweat from his brow with the back of
his arm. 'It saved this farm, that's what it did.' He looked
round him. 'This place'll come back eventually. Drain the
land and the right grasses'll grow : fertilize, slag, shove the
dung and the slurry back on, and the grasses'll grow like
mad. Buy in fresh cows, use premium bulls, enlarge the
herd . . . It'll come.'

'What are you going to do about the shoot?'

'Let it to anyone who's fool enough to pay good money
for it. Meantime, I'll clear as many acres of the woods as I
can for more fields.'

'You've got it all planned out, then?'

'I've had it planned a long time. And when I saw that
bloody old fool raping the soil . . .' He stopped.

'You wished him dead?'

'Dead and buried,' said Hulton violently, 'so as the land
could come to me. It hurt to see the land being ruined.'

Hulton had wanted the farm right enough, thought Clayton, but as he had said to Akers, Hulton's reason wasn't
entirely selfish—as a true countryman, he had been genu-
inely distressed by seeing land become derelict.

Hulton wiped his forehead again, then looked at his
watch. 'I'll be getting back to work : another hour'll see this
field done. There's so much to do.' He climbed back on to
the tractor.

'There's something more I want to know,' said Clayton.
'What?' He pushed in the tractor's stop button.

'Where were you at three in the afternoon on Monday?'

'What's that? The time when the old fool was getting his chips?'

'Yes.'

'D'you think I might have shot the old bastard?'

'That's your suggestion.'

'I'll tell you, whenever I came over here and saw what he was doing to the place I could've choked the bloody daylights out of him.'

'So now tell me where you were.'

'Making hay for old Fingle—who was told as a boy you shouldn't ever cut for hay until the middle of August and who never allowed anyone to teach him differently.'

'Can you prove you were there?'

'Ask him.'

'Did he see you at three o'clock, then?'

Hulton's heavy forehead creased. 'He was around earlier some time, then I saw him at half-past three. I'd stopped cutting and he came up and asked me why I was stopped. I told him, if he wanted his bloody cows milked, I had to.'

'How far's that farm from here?'

'Thirty miles, near enough.' Hulton started the tractor. He backed to the edge of the ditch, lowered the mole, and engaged second low.

Clayton watched the tractor moving slowly but inexorably forward, dragging the mole which was shattering the ground several inches below the surface. There must be a primeval satisfaction from tilling the land, he thought, a satisfaction that came from doing something wholly constructive, wholly beneficial.

He walked back to the house and was greeted by the barking of the dogs at the rear. As he knocked on the front door, he wondered what Mrs Knott would do with them—

she didn't strike him as a woman who had much love for animals.

There was no answer to his knock. Mrs Knott had said there probably wouldn't be and he'd find the key under a brick by the front door.

He went in and upstairs to the bedroom she had identified as her husband's. He searched it, but found nothing of any significance. He went into the other four bedrooms and the bathroom, all small and, he was certain, far different from the kind of rooms she had imagined she would inhabit as Mrs Knott of Knott Farm.

Downstairs, the two original houses had not been thrown together so that to get from one side to the other one had either to go outside or upstairs and along to the second stairs. The two sitting-rooms were poky and the furnishings had become very worn. Leading off the smaller sitting-room was what had obviously once been the larder and this had been turned into a gunroom—a very grand description for what was virtually just a dark closet. Inside was a gun cupboard and he opened this. A twelve-bore, a four-ten, and a two-two stood in the racks and on the shelf above there was cleaning equipment, cartridge bag, and a cartridge belt. He took out the twelve-bore. It had the balance of a top-quality sidelock and when he checked the maker he saw it was a Churchill. How much had that cost? How many fields had not been slagged and fertilized because Knott had bought it? He replaced the gun and shut the cupboard. On top was a cardboard carton and he brought it down and looked inside. There were eight boxes of cartridges, seven a light browny-red in colour and one green. He returned the carton. He'd never shot. He couldn't understand the pleasure some people seemed to gain from shooting living animals although, equally, he didn't condemn the sport out of hand.

He checked the far two ground-floor rooms. One was an

office and the other was an untidy workshop. The office clearly hadn't been used for months : on the table were some papers covered in dust and these were dated the previous November.

He returned upstairs and went down to the front door he had entered by. He locked up and replaced the key under the brick and thought what an obvious hiding-place this would be to any housebreaker.

He drove off, cutting through the lanes to pick up the main road to Abbotsbridge and Trighton.

Clayton arrived at No. 5, Dock Road, at the same moment as a blonde and he introduced himself to Hazel Clews. She seemed flustered by the meeting, but in his experience most people remembered their latest peccadilloes whenever introduced to a detective.

Morris had been right, thought Clayton, she really did exude sex. Every movement of her shapely body drew attention to it in a lascivious manner. Margery would have named her tart within seconds of meeting.

She opened the front door, shouted to her mother, and led the way into the front room. She sat down and her very short skirt rode higher up her thigh. She tugged at it in a way that made it seem almost as if she were caressing her own flesh.

'I just want to clear up a point or two,' Clayton said. 'You know that it's now been confirmed Daniel Knott died in the fire?'

'Yes.' She showed no emotion.

'You were having an affair with him?'

'He wouldn't leave me alone.'

'Did you know he was married?'

'That was his business.'

'Did his wife know of your relationship with him?'

'Give over,' she said scornfully.

She was tough, brought up in a tough school of life. She

had seen Knott as a dirty old man who desperately wanted her and was ready to pay for her favours: she would never have considered the wife's misery. 'Can you be quite certain she didn't know of your existence?'

'If you'd seen how scared he was to take me anywhere he might run into her, you wouldn't ask.'

'Whereabouts did he take you?'

'Up to the big smoke, mainly.'

'How often did you see him?'

'Too often. He wouldn't leave me alone.'

'If that's what you thought, why go out with him at all?'

'Why d'you think?' She sneered.

He regretfully gave her some credit for her unabashed honesty. 'Did he ever tell you about the life insurance he'd taken out that named you the beneficiary?'

'No.'

'When did you first hear about it?'

'I read it in the papers.'

'Are you quite certain of that?'

'He didn't tell me.' Her voice had become slightly shrill.

'Forty thousand pounds is a lot of money.'

She began to chew her lower lip between her even white teeth. She uncrossed her legs and instinctively his gaze was attracted. There was an animal magnetism about her that a man in his forties, married to a woman who was inclined to be frigid, would find irresistible.

'When's the money mine?' she suddenly asked.

'I've no idea.'

'They've got to pay up quick, haven't they?'

'Why not ask them?'

She looked at him. 'Are you sure it's forty thousand quid?'

'That's what the manager of the insurance company said.'

She began to fidget with the outsize loop of the zip fastener which ran right down the front of her dress. With a sense of shocked irritation, he suddenly found he was imagining what it would be like to pull the zip down. 'You haven't expressed very much sorrow at his death,' he said harshly.

'I'm not crying myself sick. The only thing he did for me was to take me to places.'

'And put you down for forty thousand quid when he died.'

She ran her tongue slowly around her full lips.

'Did he ever mention the farm?'

She shook her head. 'No.'

'You'd no idea how it was doing?'

'Look, he didn't talk about it when he was with me. Why should he?'

Why indeed? he thought. 'Where were you at three o'clock Monday afternoon?'

'At work.'

'Can you prove that?'

'Ask the old bitch who runs the shop. Went at me all ends up for being late back from lunch, then started all over again because a friend dropped in for a chat. That was near three.'

'Who was this friend?'

'What's it to you?'

'Information.'

'It ain't none of your business.'

'Male or female?'

She was silent.

'I'll be seeing the manageress when I leave here.'

'Male,' she answered sullenly.

'The same male who visited you when my detective-sergeant came here?'

'What if it was?'

'What's his name?'

'Find out.'

'What's the matter—has he got a record?'

'You bastards never let alone, do you?' she shouted.

'What's his name?'

She hesitated, then said: 'Alf Shear.'

'Go around with him much?'

'Sometimes.'

'Did you see much of him when you were going about with Daniel Knott?'

'No.'

'Would you call it a recent friendship?'

She stared at him with hatred.

He stood up. 'Thanks for your help.'

'I ain't helped you.'

No, he thought as he left, she hadn't. If her evidence and Hulton's was corroborated, each of the three persons who benefited from Knott's death had a good alibi for the time of death. In that case, Akers had to be right—the odd scraps of curious evidence were meaningless.

CHAPTER XI

CLAYTON KNOCKED on the front door of No. 36, Hammerton Road, and it was opened by Mrs Wade. Pritchard had said she was a slice of desiccated coconut and he was not inclined to argue with that description. He introduced himself and she said, sharply, that she'd been more than enough troubled already and all that the police seemed to be interested in was getting her a bad name in the district. It was with a very ill grace that she let him into the house.

Alexander's bedroom was undergoing a spring clean : the bed was stripped, the curtains and carpet were missing, and the walls had recently been washed down.

She stood just inside the room, arms crossed. 'When are you going to take all his things away?'

'As soon as possible, Mrs Wade, but so far we've been unable to locate his sister.'

'You're the police, aren't you? You ought to be able to do a simple thing like that.'

'I'm afraid it's not all that easy,' he answered pacifically.

'As I've always said, when you call on the police to do something for you, they say they can't.'

'Unfortunately, we don't even know her married name.'

'Well I'm telling you, I've got to have this room emptied and clean to let to someone else.'

He hurriedly began to search the room. Margery had always said he was no match for a shrewish woman, being unable to be rude enough.

'What are you looking for?' she demanded suddenly.

'His washing tackle.'

'In the top left-hand drawer of the chest-of-drawers.' She uncrossed her arms and pointed.

He pulled open the indicated drawer. Inside was a sponge bag, which contained soap and flannel, a tin of denture cleaner, a safety razor, a tube of shaving cream and a pair of metal-backed hair brushes and comb. He closed the drawer. 'Where did he keep his medicine?'

'If there's nothing in any of the drawers, he didn't have any. I wouldn't allow anything anywhere else.'

He searched the other drawers and found no medicine.

Curiosity made her ask him, in a slightly more pleasant voice : 'Are you looking for something special, then?'

'I wondered if he'd some sleeping tablets. Did you ever see any empty medicine bottles in his waste-paper basket?'

'No.'

He stood in the centre of the room. 'Would you always have known when he left the house and when he returned?'

'I did not spy on him.'

He assured her that nothing had been further from his thoughts.

She appeared to be mollified. 'He had a key to the front door and let himself in and out when he wanted. I'm a sound sleeper and his comings and goings never worried me.'

'What kind of time did he leave in the mornings?'

'He was usually very early. He was always telling me that in his job it was the early bird who caught all the worms.'

'Could there have been times when he got back here after you'd gone to bed and then he'd already left in the morning when you got up?'

'That happened.' She thrust forward her angular chin. 'But that's not to say I waste my time lying in bed of a morning.'

Lying in bed in the morning was a Sybaritic pleasure and therefore he was sure she had never ever indulged in it. 'Did you give him breakfast when he wasn't away early?'

'That's right.'

'How often did this happen?'

'Not very often. He usually left early.'

'What about the other meals?'

'He made his own arrangements.'

'Did you see him on Monday?'

'He came back to the house around lunchtime and said he'd forgotten some papers: went up to his room for them.'

'Have you any idea exactly what time this would have been?'

'He left again at half-past one.'

'Did you by any chance see him leave?'

'I was tidying up the hall when he came downstairs and went out.'

'I don't suppose you'd have noticed whether he was wearing gloves?'

'Of course he wasn't. Not in that heat,' she said scornfully.

'Are you quite sure?'

'Yes.'

The journey need only have taken half an hour, he

thought, but the van had not arrived at the farm until a quarter past two. Was there any significance in this?

Clayton was in his office at five that afternoon when Akers came in, crossed to the second desk, and sat down. He looked at Clayton. 'I've been expecting a report from you,' he said sharply.

'I tried to contact you earlier on, sir, but they said you were out at the farm.'

'I've been back a long time now.'

'As a matter of fact, I took a quick trip up to Relstone to see Mrs Wade.'

'Why?'

'I wanted to check if there were any signs of barbiturates amongst Alexander's effects. My DC hadn't reported finding any, but I reckoned he might have overlooked their importance.'

'What did you discover?'

'There were no medicines of any sort and Mrs Wade said there were never any empty medicine bottles in the waste-paper basket . . . That's odd, you know,' said Clayton thoughtfully. 'A bloke who takes barbiturates usually has a store of them. Another thing, he wasn't wearing gloves when he left and the journey took him fifteen minutes longer than it need have done. Fifteen minutes surely isn't long enough for him to have visited another farm . . .'

'Have you considered the possibility of heavy traffic or his doing a spot of shopping?' Akers rested his elbows on the desk and placed his fingertips together. 'Did you by any chance manage to find the time to do the two small things I told you to?'

'Yes, sir.'

'Then may we now leave the non-essentials and hear the results of your inquiries?'

'Both parties offered alibis. One of my DCs is checking

out Hulton's, I followed up Hazel Clews's. Hers is corroborated.'

'If all three parties have an alibi, would you agree that none of them can have had anything to do with the deaths?'

'On the face of it . . .'

'Did you go to Relstone before or after you'd questioned Hulton and Miss Clews?'

'After.'

'Then would you not agree that the question of whether or not Alexander had an entire pharmacopoeia in his room was of supreme irrelevance?'

'But I'm not certain . . .'

'Another feeling, another break in the rhythm, Inspector?'

'Yes, sir,' said Clayton doggedly.

Akers stood up. He began to pace the floor, turning smartly at the same spot each time. 'I fail to understand how a man in your position . . .' He stopped and slowly shook his head. 'I shan't be in Gertfinden much longer.'

Clayton tried to maintain a neutral expression.

'But before I go, I'd like to tell you something that might help you in the future if you take it to heart. The most important attribute which distinguishes an expert from the . . . the all-rounder . . . is his ability to appreciate simplicity. Conversely, the attribute which most distinguishes the all-rounder from the expert is his insistence on complicating everything.'

'But don't you think . . .' began Clayton.

'What?' snapped Akers angrily.

'Nothing, sir.' To mention the cow cake now would surely be the height of folly.

Margery had made a Quiche Lorraine and she had naturally expected her husband to appreciate it. However, when he ate he stared blankly into space and said nothing.

'Jim, what's wrong?' she asked in a worried tone of voice.

He looked at her. 'Why should anything be wrong?'

'Because you haven't the vaguest notion of what you're eating—and that's certainly not like you.'

He apologized. 'I'm sorry. It's the Knott case—got me tied up in knots.'

'You obviously weren't always going to be able to miss out on that pun! What's happened? Has that horrible superintendent been troubling you again? Why doesn't he go on back to London?'

'He says he very soon will be.'

'Good riddance to bad rubbish.'

'And when he leaves, he'll go convinced I'm a bone-headed country bumpkin.'

She spoke indignantly. 'Who the hell cares a fig what he thinks?'

'The trouble is, on the face of it he's right.' He slowly ate a mouthful, then said : 'What would be your reactions if I told you that it's absolutely clear what happened, that it couldn't have happened in any other way, but I've a feeling it did.'

'Can you tell me more?'

He briefly gave her all the facts.

She spoke seriously. 'Jim, you've always disliked people who are very self-satisfied—are you absolutely sure you aren't banging your head against a brick wall just to try and prove the superintendent wrong?'

'That would be damned childish,' he said, almost petulantly.

'And you can be quite childish at times. Jim, if the three of them can't have had anything to do with the deaths, that's an end of it.'

'I know.'

'Then why are you going on and on?'

'Margery, can you remember what Monday was like?'

She thought back. 'Wasn't it gloriously hot?'

'It was, yet Alexander had a lunch of meat, dumplings,

and greens. Can you imagine eating that in such a temperature?'

'I can't, but people have the oddest habits.'

He shook his head, a puzzled expression on his face.

At ten-fifteen the next morning, Clayton telephoned Louthy Products' head office and spoke to the manager. 'D'you remember that the last time I rang you, you told me Alexander was a good salesman and had put up sales in all areas except one?'

'Yes.'

'Can you tell me which area was the exception?'

'I'll have to check the records.'

Clayton waited.

'Hullo, Inspector. The area he failed in was the Gertfinden one—it extends roughly down to the coast and half-way to Abbotsbridge. Instead of sales going up ten per cent, they went down considerably.'

'Were the orders he did obtain in the Gertfinden area mainly for magnesium-enriched cow cake?'

'That's odd, they were. But how did you come to guess that?'

'It was just a thought,' replied Clayton. 'Can you let me have a look at his National Insurance card and PAYE records?'

'No, I can't,' replied the manager shortly.

'How's that?'

'As I mentioned to you before, he was paid solely on commission and was therefore self-employed so he looked after his own stamps and income tax.'

'Self employed even though he worked for you?'

'Yes.' There was a pause. 'It's the SET tax,' said the manager, his tone of voice defensive.

'How d'you mean?'

'You've never met such bureaucratic stupidity . . . Look, Inspector, it's like this. If one of our salesmen sells food

made up by us, we get the SET tax repaid : if he sells food
made up by one of the other firms whose products we
handle, we don't. Can you imagine the book-keeping and
the time we could waste sorting that lot out? In any case,
profit margins are much too low now, with farmers doing
so badly, for us to be able to afford SET on all our salesmen.
So we make 'em self-employed and don't pay a wage, but
give very good commission. Like that, there's no bother
about SET. I assure you we talked it over with our lawyers
. . .'

'I'm not worried,' cut in Clayton. 'If anyone can kick
SET in the teeth, I'm for him.' He began to tap on the desk
with his fingers. Unless he was as stupid as Akers believed
him to be, Alexander had never existed.

CHAPTER XII

CLAYTON WALKED into Morris's room. The detective-sergeant was typing out a report. 'Leave that and find the
folder of missing persons for me.'

'It should be in the filing cabinet in your room, sir.'

'I know where it should be. I also know where it isn't.'

'Mr Akers told me that when I'd finished this . . .'

'Mr Akers will have to wait.'

Morris's expression became sullen.

Clayton returned to his room and sat down. Would the
missing persons list answer his questions? He picked up the
latest crime sheet, read it quickly, remembered little of what
he'd read and replaced it. He lit a cigarette. He began to
doodle on a sheet of scrap paper. The telephone rang and he
received a report on a newly discovered breaking and entering in south-west Gertfinden. He detailed Burrows to go
out to the warehouse, then resumed his doodling.

Even Margery, who usually believed in him quite blindly,
had wondered whether he were being pig-headed simply

because he didn't like Akers. There were times, he knew, when an odd and unwelcome quirk in his character made him defend an untenable position, even while knowing it was untenable, but this was not one of those times. Experience had taught him that crime and criminals worked with a rhythm and when something turned up to upset that rhythm, something was wrong.

Morris came into his room and handed him a thick loose-leaf folder in which were the lists of missing persons over the last twelve months. Reading this was, for him, always very depressing. How much tragedy, how many heartaches, were hidden in the names and addresses? What did a family do when one of them vanished without trace? How did one live with a situation in which confirmation of death might in the end almost be called a relief?

His stubby forefinger came to a halt. Corporal White, aged 45, six feet tall, fair hair, blue eyes, no special distinguishing features. An army cook, he had left Tintham Barracks, Relstone, on March 3 for week-end leave and had disappeared. The civil authorities had been asked on April 14 to try to trace him, but without result. He was married, but separated from his wife.

Clayton resumed reading through the list until he reached the previous July, which was the last month. Only twice did he stop further to consider other disappearances. He closed the folder with a snap. This looked promising, but sometimes people reappeared and no one bothered to inform the police, sometimes the police were informed but procedure went askew and the records weren't altered.

He telephoned Tintham Barracks and spoke to the duty officer.

'Corporal White? Yes, I remember him. He's the chap who left on week-end leave and has never been heard of since.'

'Can you give me any idea of the circumstances of his disappearance?'

'I'm afraid not.'

'If I drive up right away can I see someone who can give me the details?'

'That can certainly be arranged. D'you think you know something about him, then?'

'Maybe. That's what I want to check.'

Clayton braked to a halt at the sentry-post and spoke through the opened window. The sentry jerked his thumb to his right and said the orderly room was the second shed along, then resumed his former slumped and bored stance. The army, thought Clayton, was certainly not what it had been. He drove along the road and parked by a long wooden shed around which ran a well-cut lawn and perfectly weeded flower-bed.

Lieutenant Masters was young, energetic, and friendly. He called for coffee, offered cigarettes, and promised all the help he could give.

'Can you tell me how much you've been able to find out about Corporal White?' asked Clayton.

'Sure.' The lieutenant picked up a sheet of paper. 'He was a busted sergeant who'd climbed back up to corporal—the records say he was a damned good cook, but liked the bottle. He was married, but separated from his wife : there don't seem to have been any divorce proceedings and he made a full marriage allotment. He was granted week-end leave from sixteen hundred hours on the third of March to eight hundred on the sixth. He signed out at sixteen twenty-eight. I've got the leave book for you . . .' The lieutenant pushed across a thick, solidly bound book.

Clayton looked briefly at the relevant entry. A private came in with the coffee, put the two cups on the desk, and left.

The lieutenant pushed a cup across. 'That's the end of the story as far as we're concerned. He didn't come back Monday morning and at first he was just regarded as

AWOL. Later, full inquiries were put in hand and you blokes were asked for help.'

'Any chance you can tell me what was served here for lunch that Friday?'

'What?' said the lieutenant, in astonishment.

'If you can find out what he ate for lunch it will help a lot since we know from the contents of the stomach what our dead man ate a short time before he died.'

'Are you saying you've just discovered that now, in August?'

'That's right.'

'You're welcome to your job!' The lieutenant picked up the nearer of the telephones on his desk, asked for the catering department, and told the man at the other end what he wanted.

'There's another thing,' said Clayton, 'could you get hold of one of his pals, someone who'd have known quite a bit about him?'

'Sure.' The lieutenant made a second call.

Clayton stubbed out his cigarette and drank the last of the institutional-tasting coffee. He heard the measured stamp of feet and, looking out through the window, saw a squad of men marching along. The army would never have suited him as a career—to him, one of life's most precious gifts was not to be one of the herd.

The lieutenant asked him questions about his work and showed a macabre interest in certain features of it—an interest that Clayton was not fully able to satisfy. How long was it before a corpse stank, did a drowned man sink to the bottom, could arsenic be traced in the nails of a poisoned person . . . Who, wondered Clayton, was he hoping to bludgeon, drown, or poison?

There was a sharp knock on the door. A sergeant came in, marched to the front of the desk, stamped his feet, handed over a plastic-bound book, then left, with crashing movements.

The lieutenant leafed through the pages of the book. 'Here we are . . . Breakfast: porridge and eggs and bacon. That porridge sets just like concrete. Luncheon: Windsor soup, boiled beef, dumplings, cabbage, jam tart and custard.'

'Thank you very much,' said Clayton.

The lieutenant looked up. 'You sound as if you've found out something really important?'

'I think I probably have.'

'Does it mean you've discovered what happened to the corporal?'

'Almost certainly, yes.'

'And he's dead?'

'Yes.'

The lieutenant closed the book. 'It's the first time I've ever known that what I've eaten could be important. Bit off-putting to think of someone poking through my stomach.'

There was a telephone call and in the middle of this a private reported. Studying the private, Clayton quickly came to the conclusion that he was the epitome of the old sweat: his whole expression and the way he held himself made it clear that he knew the exact limits to which he could take insolence and disobedience before he was in trouble.

The lieutenant finished his telephone call. He spoke to the private. 'The detective-inspector wants to ask you a few questions, Eastling.'

Eastling looked quickly at Clayton, then away, and his expression became quite blank. He was, thought Clayton, trying hard not to think of all the fiddles that he'd been engaged on which could be of interest to the civil police. 'I gather you knew Corporal White?' said Clayton.

'Yes, sir.'

'Did you know him well?'

'Reasonably well, sir.'

'Then I'd like your help in tracing out a few facts about him.'

Satisfied he was in no personal danger, Eastling relaxed. He spoke to Clayton in a 'matey' voice and no longer bothered to add 'sir'. 'I'll tell you what I can, but Steve was a bit of a loner, 'cept when he was on the booze. He was a proper lad then, and no mistake.'

'Can you remember if you'd any idea where he was going on the Friday he disappeared?'

Eastling scratched his neck as he thought back. 'As far as I can remember, he was going up to the smoke. He'd a Judy what he used to stay with. He showed me her photo and she wasn't no oil painting, that's for sure.'

'How was he intending to travel up to London?'

'Hitch-hike, same as always. Never took him longer than three hours.'

'Did White wear false teeth?'

'Did he wear false choppers?' Eastling scratched his head. 'I can't rightly remember . . . Now that makes me a liar. It was him what had his last eight teeth out in one day and wangled . . . and was granted a week's sick leave.'

'D'you know where he'd have had his teeth extracted?'

'Here, in camp.'

'Is the dentist in camp today?'

'Hard to say, today being Sunday. Some blokes gets Sundays off,' he said mournfully.

Clayton asked the lieutenant to find out whether the dentist was in camp. After several calls, the latter contacted a sergeant who said he was the only one from that department in the camp. The sergeant was ordered to the office with the necessary records.

Clayton questioned Eastling about whether he had ever hitch-hiked to London, but Eastling denied he had. Clayton then tried to discover whether other men who had hitch-hiked had ever commented on being picked up by a Bentley, but Eastling was unable to help.

The sergeant, in civilian clothes, reported to the office. Clayton handed him the false teeth which had come from

H

'Alexander's' body. 'Is there any chance you could identify these?'

The sergeant examined the dentures, then opened the file he had brought with him. After a short while, he said: 'These are Corporal White's, sir.'

Clayton leaned back in the chair. Detective-Superintendent Akers was not, he thought with satisfaction, going to be amused.

CHAPTER XIII

AKERS AND BODMIN were having lunch at the Three Bells. Since the county had to pay his living expenses, Akers had chosen a very good meal: prawn cocktail, fillet steak, and sherry trifle with cream (1/6 extra). To drink, he had a bottle of Gevrey-Chambertin and he had forgotten to refill Bodmin's glass.

' 'Afternoon, Clayton,' said Akers, with unaccustomed warmth. He spooned up the last of the trifle from the glass dish. 'We're having coffee soon, so sit down and join us in a cup.'

Clayton sat down.

'You know, for a town like Gertfinden, this isn't a bad little hotel,' said Akers patronizingly. 'The beds are comfortable and the food's not bad.'

The menu was in front of Clayton. He started to read through it and immediately felt twice as hungry.

'Being on call to the whole of the country,' went on Akers, 'we're always travelling and spending time in hotels and some of them are hotels only in name. Still, that's one of the penalties of being an expert who's needed here, there, and the other place.'

What a pity he hadn't been needed there or the other place, thought Clayton.

'But this is the age of the expert, the man who specializes

and deals with the problems the ordinary person is unable to cope with.' Akers smiled. 'I know you blokes in the local forces don't like our doing the work, out of some sort of mistaken sense of county loyalty, but the hard fact is, you just can't cope on your own.'

'You're probably right, sir,' said Clayton, 'yet in our own muddled way we do pick up the odd scrap of information on such things as cow cake.'

Much of Akers's geniality disappeared and the hard, scornful expression returned to his face. 'Are you trying to be funny?'

'No, sir.'

'Then I'm sorry to say it seems you're quite incapable of appreciating which are the important points of a case and which are the totally unimportant ones.'

'Possibly. But once in a blue moon we manage to get an idea that's good.'

Akers began to finger a piece of the inside of his roll. His expression became wary. 'Just what have you come here to say?'

'I had a word with the manager of Louthy Products to find out in which area it was that Alexander failed to increase sales.'

'And?'

'That area was the Gertfinden one.'

Akers beckoned to a waiter. He ordered coffee and three cognacs, not bothering to ask whether Clayton and Bodmin liked cognac. 'Has anything else turned up?' He dropped the pellet of bread and began to roll another.

'Yes, sir.'

'What?'

'I got to wondering about missing persons and checked through the lists. I came across a Corporal White who disappeared in March. He left the army camp in Relstone for week-end leave on March the third and almost certainly set out to hitch-hike to London.'

The waiter brought them coffee and the wine waiter came across with three very large balloon glasses in each of which was a very small measure of cognac. The waiter left.

Akers helped himself to cream and sugar. 'What do we know about this Corporal White?' he asked casually. He passed the cream and sugar to Clayton.

Clayton gave himself two spoonfuls of sugar and then rather guiltily added a third one. He was also generous with the cream. 'Do you remember, sir, my saying that it seemed very odd that Alexander had eaten a meal of meat, dumplings, and greens, on one of the hottest days in August?'

'Of course.'

Clayton spoke triumphantly. 'Corporal White ate a meal of Windsor soup, boiled beef, dumplings, and greens, on the third of March.'

'I see,' said Akers, as if he'd been told nothing of significance.

'I showed a member of the dental staff at the camp the plates we found by Alexander's body. They've been identified as Corporal White's.'

Akers dropped the second bread pellet on to the plate. A waiter came to clear the table, but was waved away. 'You've been very busy, Inspector,' he said.

Clayton felt bitterly disappointed. Akers showed no discernible emotion of anger or annoyance.

Akers picked up his balloon glass and cradled it in his right hand, holding it near his nose the better to enjoy the bouquet. 'We may now assume that the second body in the fire was Corporal White's,' he said, as if he had been considering the matter for a long time and had at last been able to come to a judicial conclusion.

'Which means . . .' began Clayton, speaking rather more loudly than he usually did.

'Which means,' interrupted Akers smoothly, 'that either he lived until Monday and had a lunch on that day which was by coincidence the same as he ate in March, or he's been dead for six months and both his body and his stomach contents escaped decay. The first explanation calls for a very great coincidence, the second, an apparent impossibility.'

'Not if you remember . . .' began Clayton.

'But it is not impossible,' continued Akers smoothly, 'if we remember there was a deep-freeze at the farm, destroyed by the fire.'

Clayton stared angrily at the table.

'Do we know the size of that deep-freeze?' asked Akers.

'Yes.'

'What was it?'

'Sixteen cubic feet.'

'Enough both for the body and the dog meat on top which concealed it.'

Akers sipped his brandy, Bodmin drank his in three hasty gulps. Clayton suffered a strong desire to throw his over the detective-superintendent.

'Corporal White,' said Akers authoritatively, 'was picked up by Knott when he was trying to hitch-hike to London. Knott murdered him—probably by drugging him and, when unconscious, stifling him with a plastic bag over his head. Knott took the body to the farm and fitted it into the deep-freeze, which preserved it until wanted. Proof of this lies in the medical evidence of asphyxiation before being affected by the fire, the last meal eaten, and the dental plate . . . Would you like a cigar, Inspector?'

'I'll stick to cigarettes,' Clayton said grittily, even though he loved cigars.

Akers beckoned to the head waiter, who came straight across and then called over a second waiter with a box containing a selection of cigars. Akers chose a Corona Extra and the head waiter cut the end for him.

When they were alone, Akers said : 'We now come to the problem of the real motive behind all this. It's pretty obvious, isn't it, Inspector?'

'Is it?'

'Surely, we're faced by a crime within a crime? Daniel Knott set out to swindle the Riverside Insurance Company by taking out a large life insurance, payable to his girl-friend in the event of his death. His intention was to fake his own death, wait until Hazel Clews had been paid the forty thousand, and then he and she would go away and live happily on the money. Since he wasn't a fool, he knew that when a man takes out a large insurance policy and "dies" shortly afterwards, the insurance company auto-matically becomes suspicious. So he decided to try to avert, or divert, such suspicions. He reasoned, rightly, that if it appeared he'd been murdered rather than accidentally killed or had committed suicide, there was little chance of his faked death coming to light since all the police's efforts would be directed towards finding the murderer and not to uncover-ing a possible fraud.

'He needed someone of his own age, height, and general appearance, without peculiar physical characteristics, who wore false teeth. He picked up an unknown number of hitch-hikers before he found Corporal White. He killed the corporal, carried him back to Knott Farm, and preserved him in the deep-freeze. His next job was to invent Alex-ander and give him substance and an existence because if Knott was to be murdered there had to be a murderer. Do you follow, that, Inspector?'

Clayton didn't answer.

Akers held the cigar between thumb and all four fingers and drew on it with deep pleasure. 'Louthy advertised in the papers for a traveller,' he continued, 'and Knott applied for the post and was granted an interview. He disguised him-self in the simplest way—a toupee to transform his baldness into a good head of hair, a moustache to provide a pro-minent facial feature, and pads in his mouth to fill out his rather hollow cheeks, but nothing more elaborate than that.

This change in appearance would be sufficient to deceive anyone who didn't know him really well. He found digs in Relstone and then, to explain his frequent and prolonged absences, invented a sister with whom he frequently stayed and he also made a habit of apparently leaving the house very early in the morning. Obviously, most of the time he left the digs in the middle of the night and returned to a wife who believed he'd been out with Hazel Clews.

'Oddly enough, he made a good commercial traveller, increasing sales except in the one area he dare not work at all hard because there he might meet people who would see through his disguise. To cover up what was going on, however, he made up fictitious orders for cow cake from farmers in the Gertfinden area and collected these orders from the central distribution point in his van, paid for them in the names of other farmers, and stored the cake on his own place. You'll remember that one of the odd points we noted early on was the excess of cow cake in the barn?'

Clayton tried to say a number of things at the same time.

Akers continued to speak smoothly. 'A murder needs a motive and so Knott had to produce a motive for his own murder—he also needed to find the money to pay for all the cow cake he didn't want. Hence, the fertilizer subsidy swindle.

'The scene was ready to be set.' Akers gently scraped the ash from his cigar into an ash-tray. 'The body was taken out of the deep-freeze and thawed. Knott's wife was spending all day and every day with Miss Corrins and Browland was paid only to do the milking so no one was around the farm during the day. Knott left the farm—on foot—picked up the van which he must have hidden in the woods, drove to his digs to show himself there, then returned to the farm. He left the van on the concrete after wiping it clear of prints and made certain the papers in it would lead us to the fertilizer swindle.

'He went through to the store-room where the electrical wiring was known to be in a terrible state and where there were diesel oil and paraffin to create a blaze which would burn the body far beyond physical recognition. He prepared to switch a set of his false teeth into the body of the thawed Corporal White because they provided one of the best means of identification . . . How do you see that things went now, Inspector?'

'Surely you know?' said Clayton, with furious sarcasm.

'It always helps to have a check,' replied Akers blandly.

Clayton stubbed out his cigarette with unnecessary force.

'Well?' said Akers.

'It's obvious someone else knew what was going on and joined in. He or she used the set-up provided by Knott to shoot Knott and set the place on fire so that it looked like an "enclosed" murder brought on by a row over the swindle.'

Akers finished his cognac and put the glass down on the table. 'That's the picture,' he agreed.

'Sir . . .' began Clayton.

'Something troubling you?' asked Akers, a mocking expression in his eyes.

'Do you by any chance remember . . .'

'I wonder if you're about to remind me of some of the things I said to you?' Akers smiled. 'My dear Clayton, I long ago discovered that a man works best when he feels he has a challenge to meet—and so I gave you the challenge and the spur of my apparent disbelief.' He stood up. 'I think we'll have a conference at the police station in half an hour's time.'

'In half an hour's time I shall be eating my lunch,' said Clayton rudely.

'You haven't eaten, yet? Good heavens, you must be hungry! Shall we say in one hour, then?' He left.

Bodmin spoke lugubriously. 'Will it help, sir, if I tell you that this sort of thing's happened before?'

'No,' said Clayton bitterly, 'I'm quite certain it won't.'

Clayton looked across the kitchen table at Margery. 'The worst thing of all is that that bastard has reduced me to the state when I'm even ready to believe he might have suspected the truth after all.'

'I'm quite certain he didn't do anything of the sort,' she said loyally.

'When I remember all the lectures he gave me on ignoring non-essential details . . . When I remember all the times he said the cow cake was of absolutely no consequence . . . When I remember all the times he told me I was a country simpleton for thinking a heavy meal on a hot day was of any importance . . . I could strangle him with my own hands.'

'Don't get too het-up, love,' she pleaded. 'After all, does it really matter who discovered the truth so long as it's discovered—you've always told me police work is a team effort?'

'Traitress,' he cried.

She smiled. 'What is it, Jim, are you after a medal?'

'You know me better than that.'

'Yes,' she answered, and suddenly there was a touch of sadness to her voice. 'You wouldn't have gone on and on from any sense of personal glorification—more's the pity.' More ambition and how high could he not have risen? she wondered. Yet more ambition and would he have been the same warm, loving husband?— 'You did it because you believe in truth.'

He stood up, pushing his chair back, and began to pace the floor. 'By God, he's a . . . a shark.'

She was near enough to him to grip his hand. 'I thought you were going to say something very different! Jim, take a word of advice. Next time, just listen and don't try to help. He's not the only shark in the world.'

'Don't worry, this case has taught me one thing—from now on, I'm just not talking!'

CHAPTER XIV

THE HEAT had become oppressive, although the sky was overcast, and the air had the sullen, trapped feeling that so often presaged a thunderstorm. The window in Clayton's room was wide open, but the place was airless. Clayton had taken off his coat, but the sweat ran down his face, as it did on Bodmin's: only Akers remained cool, by some alchemy known only to himself.

Akers stood in the centre of the room. 'There is an old aphorism,' he said, 'that in a motivated murder you look for the person who had the greatest motive and there you have the murderer.'

Akers, thought Clayton, had the knack of saying the obvious, yet making it seem freshly discovered truth. Perhaps all success was a confidence trick.

'What motives have we?' said Akers. He raised his right hand and flicked up the forefinger. 'First, forty thousand pounds: due to Hazel Clews as the beneficiary under the life insurance. Second, jealousy: Mrs Knott almost certainly knew of her husband's affair. Third, the estate: Paul Hulton has never made any secret of his longing for the farm, worth close on fifty thousand with the woods. What is the greatest motive? There's little difference in this context between forty and fifty thousand pounds and jealousy is incapable of definition. For the moment, we must accept the fact that all three have the same degree of motive.

'Let us move on to opportunity. Obviously, Mrs Knott had every chance to discover her husband's intended fraud and to commit the murder. Equally, if Hazel Clews was told about the swindle, she would have known or could have found out all the details including the day and time when Knott was going to set the scene of his own murder and she could have acted on her own or, far more likely, in company with Shear. Hulton, for his part, was always turning up at the farm, trying to get Knott to farm it properly and so save some of his inheritance, and what's more likely than that he uncovered what was going on? After all, he had only to see all the cow cake in the barn for him to become suspicious, as we did.' Akers crossed to his desk, carefully hitched up his right trouser-leg, and sat down on the edge. 'We know that each of the suspects has provided an alibi for the time of the murder and we have checked these. Until we could be certain we were not dealing with an "enclosed" murder, we accepted them. Now, we know that one of them is false, as is the corroborative evidence. Our next job is to find out which one it is.'

He folded his arms across his chest. You smooth, sneaky bastard, thought Clayton.

Akers detailed Clayton to go to Trighton to see Hazel Clews and Shear while he questioned Mrs Knott and Hulton : if neither of them made any progress, they would change over. It was a basic truth of detection—surprisingly, not yet reiterated at length by Akers—that two interviews in quick succession by different interviewers offered more chance of success than several interviews by the same interviewer.

Clayton and DC Burrows drove to Trighton. Despite the threatening sky, now filled with black-bellied clouds that promised rain, there was a lot of tripper traffic in both towns and when they reached Dock Road it was over ten minutes before Clayton could find a parking space. The walk back along the road took them past the east pier and Clayton stopped to watch a cross-Channel boat set sail.

He leaned on the rails that protected pedestrians from the drop to the water. 'I wouldn't mind being on that—just think, in next to no time they'll all be in France.'

'Never fancied France myself,' said Burrows.

Clayton half turned. 'Why ever not? You can have the best food and wine in the world there.'

'It's all garlic and frogs' legs. I'd rather have a plate of bangers and mash and a pint of bitter.'

My God! thought Clayton. He could still remember the first meal he and Margery had had in Paris: a plump, delicious capon stuffed with truffles and accompanied by a magnificent sauce. Even the memory set his gastric juices flowing. 'Come on,' he said impatiently.

They threaded their way through the strolling holiday-makers and crossed the road to No. 5. Clayton knocked on the door. There was no answer. He knocked again, louder and longer. After a further wait, the door was opened by Hazel Clews and the first thing he noticed was that her dress was buttoned up wrongly, as if this had been done in a hurry.

They went inside. Alf Shear was in the front room and his face was flushed.

'Sorry to interrupt you,' said Clayton, with malicious ambiguity.

Shear didn't answer.

Unusually, he closely resembled his mug-shots, thought Clayton—smooth, mean, and smart. His face was long and thin and it held lines of hard cunning. From the way Hazel Clews looked at him, she was infatuated by him and Clayton was ready to bet this was partially because he was so hard, perhaps even cruel.

'What d'you want?' demanded Hazel Clews. She went and stood close to Shear.

'A word or two with both of you,' answered Clayton. It was noticeable that she was not as self-confident as on his last visit.

'I'm off,' said Shear.

'After you've answered a few questions.'

'You ain't stopping me going anywhere.'

'Then you'd rather we picked you up at your home or out

in the streets?' Clayton judged Shear to have a sharp temper and an automatic hatred of authority, but to be able, when necessary, to control both sufficiently coolly to assess a situation such as the present one. Shear had been found guilty of two robberies and a GBH, as well as of several lesser offences when a minor: it was a fairly safe bet that his convictions represented only a tithe of the offences he had committed.

'What's hazing you?' demanded Shear roughly.

'I'm investigating the murder of Daniel Knott.'

'So?'

'So I think you may be able to help me. Will you go into another room while I question Miss Clews?'

'Don't go,' said Hazel Clews. It was obvious that the moment she had spoken, she regretted it.

'Scared they'll jump you?' sneered Shear. 'They ain't man enough for that.' He walked across to the door, a swaggering challenge to his shoulders. He left and slammed the door shut behind himself.

Clayton sat down and nodded at Burrows to do the same. Burrows, he thought, might be unaware of things that could only be sensed, such as the exact relationship between a man and a woman but he would miss nothing of what was said and of what he saw.

Hazel Clews picked up a pack of cigarettes from the mantelpiece and lit one. She sat down on the arm of a chair, which exposed one of her legs. This time, she did not bother to affect modesty and try to draw her skirt down.

'Why can't you leave me alone?' she demanded. 'You come bustin' in on a Sunday afternoon . . .'

'Certain new evidence has come to light,' he said. He watched her expression closely.

She drew heavily on the cigarette.

'Daniel Knott was engaged in setting up an insurance swindle, the crux of which was that he intended to fake his own death and then you and he would enjoy the forty thousand.'

'I don't know nothing,' she said harshly.

Clayton looked surprised. 'He must have discussed the details with you?'

'I said, I don't know nothing.'

'I don't believe you,' remarked Clayton calmly.

She threw the half-smoked cigarette into the grate. 'All right,' she muttered, 'I knew something was on. He said as we was going away together and we'd be rich . . . But he didn't say nothing more than that.'

'You must have asked him what he meant?'

'He told me he wasn't saying nothing, then I wouldn't know nothing if things went wrong.'

'Had you agreed to go away with him?'

She plucked at one of the buttons on her dress. 'I . . . I hadn't arranged nothing definite.'

'But you'd have wanted to hang on to a share in the forty thousand?'

'Ain't I said, I didn't know nothing about that?'

Clayton nodded, as if he accepted her evidence. 'Knott was unlucky—someone discovered what he was setting-up and decided to take advantage of the fact to murder him.'

She lit another cigarette.

'You're not surprised?' asked Clayton.

'I don't know nothing.'

'You and your friend Shear could have murdered him.'

'I didn't kill him. Alf ain't never met him.'

'You had a very strong motive—forty thousand quid.'

Her voice rose. 'I keep saying, I didn't know about the money. Why keep on and on at me? Why not have a go at that bitch of a wife of his? If anyone killed him, she did.'

'Why should she have done that?'

'Why? You call yourself a detective and don't know? She was mad jealous, that's what.'

'According to what you told me before, Mrs Knott had no idea her husband was going around with you.'

She looked at him with a sudden animal wariness, as if realizing for the first time that his pleasant manner did not mean he was soft.

'You were lying to me.' He made it a statement of fact, not a question.

'I didn't want to get mixed up in nothing,' she answered surlily.

'What's the truth, then?'

'She came into a restaurant where Daniel and me was eating. When he saw her, he was shocked stupid. I thought she'd come over and row, but she never said nothing, just stood there for a bit and then walked out like the stupid bitch she is.'

Hazel Clews, thought Clayton, could never understand that Mrs Knott's one desire at that moment of shock would have been to avoid any sort of a scene because the Knotts did not have scenes. 'Which restaurant did this happen in?'

'I can't remember.'

'Try harder.'

'I tell you, I can't remember. I never bothered where he took me. If we didn't go up to London, we went miles and miles to keep out of his wife's way. It could've been anywhere.'

'Did he ever say what happened when he got home that night?'

'She rowed him and tried to find out who I was.' Her voice became scornful. 'He tried to tell her I was just the daughter of an old school friend of his. The old fool thought she'd believe him.'

'What makes you so certain that she didn't?'

'Because she came snooping to find out where I work.'

'When?'

'Just recent. I was in the shop, doing some flowers, and turns round and there she was, peering through the window and looking like an ugly old witch.'

'What day was this?'

She drew on the cigarette, then threw it into the fire-place. 'It must've been Monday.'

'Last Monday?'

'Yes.'

'How can you be certain of that?'

'It was the same day Alf came in to have a word with me and the old bitch of a manageress started shouting because of him.'

'What did Mrs Knott do once she'd seen you?'

'Gawd knows! Had a fit, like as not.'

'Why d'you say that?'

'That's how she looked—all twisted up.'

'Did you try to speak to her?'

'I ain't that stupid.'

Clayton thought for a few moments, then said: 'Thanks very much, Miss Clews. Would you like to go and ask Mr Shear to come in here now?'

She spoke loudly. 'This is my house, you know.'

'Of course. But you're being so helpful I'm sure you won't mind helping us that little bit longer by letting us have a word or two with Mr Shear in here.'

She hesitated, then left the room.

When Shear entered, he walked straight over to one of the chairs, sat down, and spread out his feet. His mouth, thick-lipped and sensuous yet at the same time hard, expressed scornful contempt.

'Have you known Miss Clews for long?' asked Clayton.

'What's it to you?' demanded Shear.

'I'd like to know.'

'Why?'

'To help me in my investigations into the murder of Daniel Knott.'

'D'you think I croaked the old bastard?'

'Did you?'

'Never met him.'

'Then there can't be any harm in answering my questions.'

Shear put his shoes up on the arm of the settee. 'I ain't got much more time to waste.'

'Nor have I,' said Clayton, with undiminished good humour, 'so we'll get down to the essentials. Where were you last Monday?'

'What's up? Someone nicked half a dollar from a gasmeter?'

'Last Monday, Daniel Knott was murdered by shooting.'

'It's one way of dying.'

'Did you shoot him?'

'No.'

'Then let's hear where you were between mid-day and four in the afternoon?'

'In Trighton.'

'Can you prove that?'

'Yeah.'

'Then go ahead.'

'Me and Hazel had a drink in a pub.'

'What time?'

'I wasn't watching the clock.'

'Try guessing.'

'It was just after she'd come out of the shop. She leaves that at half twelve.'

'How long were you in the pub?'

'Long enough.'

'How long in time?'

'Something over half an hour.'

'The name of the pub?'

'The Admiral's Head.'

'Where did you go from there?'

'We came back here.'

'Why?'

'Don't be so bloody daft.'

'Were her parents in the house?'

'No.'

'When did you leave here?'

'When it was time for her to go back to the shop.'

'What did you do after she'd returned to the shop?'

'Had a wander round town.'

'Doing what?'

'Wandering.'

'When did you next see Miss Clews?'

'When I chatted her in the shop.'

'What time was that?'

'How should I know? I ain't no time-clock.'

'Have another guess.'

'It was something after three.'

'Right, thanks very much.' Clayton stood up.

Shear, sprawled out in the chair, stared up at him with undisguised hatred.

The manageress of the flower-shop lived in a small flat half-way up the steep hill which lay immediately behind the eastern arm of the harbour. Mrs Quale was a middle-aged, solid woman with an authoritative manner. It was easy to understand why she and Hazel Clews disliked each other so much.

'As I said before, she's not the type of person I would employ if I had any choice,' said Mrs Quale. She sat upright in a hard-backed chair in the small sitting-room. 'Unfortunately, because of the high wages paid in the factories, I have very little choice in the quality of my assistants.'

It would take an angel to satisfy her, Clayton thought. 'Will you tell me again about her movements on Monday afternoon?'

Mrs Quale studied him. 'You keep asking me the same questions. Did she have something to do with the deaths?'

'The two things just don't follow,' he answered in a casual voice. 'It's merely that we have to take as much trouble establishing the innocence of the innocent as proving the guilt of the guilty.'

She looked as if she did not believe him. 'She was late back from lunch—but then there was nothing unusual in that.'

'How late?'

'She returned well after a quarter to two although she'd left the shop at half-past twelve.'

'And she was in the shop from then on?'

'That's right.'

'A man came in and spoke to her during the afternoon?'

'I thought at first he was a customer, but very soon saw he wasn't. All he wanted was to talk to her—and this was during shop hours.'

'What time was this?'

'Twenty minutes past three.'

'You seem very sure of the time?' he said.

'When I realized what he wanted, I checked with my watch to see how long he stayed.'

'Would you recognize him again?'

'Of course.'

Clayton took half a dozen photographs from his pocket and handed them to Mrs Quale. She picked out the one of Shear without any hesitation.

CHAPTER XV

AKERS LISTENED to Clayton's report and then walked across to the window of the office. He looked out for several seconds before turning round. 'Mrs Knott has just again denied she left the house in Challock Road from the time she arrived in the morning to the time she left in the evening and Miss Corrins has corroborated her evidence. Get over there right away and see what she says in the light of this evidence.'

'Yes, sir,' said Clayton.

'You told me she employed a gardener—he might be able to help.'

'I'll have a word with him.'

'That girl's evidence,' said Akers thoughtfully, 'means far more than she realizes. When she described Mrs Knott's face as all twisted up, she was obviously describing a woman who was emotionally in a totally unstable state. It doesn't need much experience to know there's no trigger to crime quicker than emotion.'

'I'm sure you're right, sir, but it does seem a bit odd . . .'

'What were you going to say?'

'Nothing, sir.'

Akers looked long and hard at Clayton, but when he saw the DI was not going to speak, he waved his right hand in a gesture of dismissal.

Clayton walked along the corridor to the CID general room and told Burrows to accompany him. They went downstairs to his car.

As Burrows sat down in the front passenger seat, he said : 'I've fixed up to go out tonight with my wife, sir.'

'So had I,' replied Clayton.

'I haven't had the chance to go out with her in the evening for a very long time.'

'Nor have I.'

Burrows lapsed into a moody silence.

Their wives, thought Clayton as he backed and turned the car, were long-suffering.

The main road was solid with holiday traffic that was returning towards London and Clayton drove through the back streets to Challock Road. Black-bellied thunder-clouds were banked high behind Miss Corrins's house and they added to that architectural extravagance an air of impending drama. Mrs Knott's Bentley was parked in the drive and it looked even shabbier than the last time he had seen it. He hated seeing a really good car fall into decay; one of his lifelong ambitions, quite unattainable, was to own one of the original Bentleys, with strap over the bonnet and outside handbrake, whose thundering, shuddering, juddering mode of progress would threaten to sweep aside any vehicle rash enough to get in the way.

He knocked on the door. Miss Corrins opened it and when she saw him her square, solid face expressed bitter anger. 'What now?' she demanded roughly. 'I've only just got rid of someone from the police. I'm not going to go on being bothered like this—I'll complain to the chief constable.'

Clayton said nothing.

'Well, what do you want?'

'A word with you and then with Mrs Knott.'

'I've nothing more to say, nothing, d'you understand?'

'I think perhaps you ought to hear the evidence that has come to hand before you make any further comment.'

She hesitated, studied his face, and then stepped to one side. They entered.

'Well?' she demanded.

'You've been asked several times whether Mrs Knott left this house at any time last Monday and you've always answered that she did not. Yet we now know she was in Trighton-on-Sea at around two o'clock that afternoon.'

Miss Corrins thrust out her formidable chin. 'She was here all day.'

'She was identified in Trighton by a person who knew her.'

'That person's lying.'

He shook his head.

'I tell you, it's a lie,' she shouted.

'Where's Mrs Knott?' he asked.

She instinctively looked at the door of the sitting-room. Realizing what she had done, she jerked her head round. 'She's gone out,' she rasped.

'Her car is still in the drive.' Clayton spoke to Burrows. 'See if Mrs Knott is in that room.'

'You've no right . . .' began Miss Corrins, but she stopped as Burrows opened the door. They could all see Mrs Knott who sat on the settle and was staring with a frightened expression at the doorway.

'Why do you keep lying to us?' asked Clayton. He was astonished to see the sudden glint of tears in Miss Corrins's eyes : he had not believed her capable of tears. She seemed about to say something, then turned and moved in an ungainly manner towards the stairs.

'Miss Corrins,' he said, 'what's the name and address of your gardener?'

She came to a stop with her hand on the banisters. 'Why d'you want to know?'

'I'm going to question him.'

'I won't tell you.'

'That just means I'll have to come back and talk to him here.'

She began to climb the stairs. 'His name's Jarrold and he lives at fourteen, Northgate Road. He'll swear Phyllis never left here,' she shouted.

He watched her go out of sight. He disliked her as a woman, yet he hated having so distressed her.

They went into the sitting-room. Mrs Knott looked almost old : she wore no make-up and her cheeks were colourless, her face haggard and deeply lined. She had a handkerchief in her hands and kept plucking at it.

Clayton stopped by one of the arm-chairs. He spoke quietly. 'Did you hear all that I said to Miss Corrins, Mrs Knott?'

She shook her head.

'I told her that we now have evidence you left this house last Monday. At about two o'clock in the afternoon, you were in Trighton.'

'No!' she cried.

'Your reason for being there was to try to identify the woman you'd seen your husband with at a restaurant.'

'He never went out with another woman.'

'He often went out with Hazel Clews, who works in a florist's.'

'That's all a lie,' she cried hoarsely.

'We have the evidence of Hazel Clews. Last Monday, she was at work when she saw you outside the shop, on the pavement. She says your face was distorted as if you were under a great emotional strain. Don't you think it's very much in your interests to tell us if you were suffering so terribly?'

She stared straight at him and just for a few seconds her fingers did not pluck at the handkerchief. 'My husband never ever went out with another woman.'

'But he took out a heavy life insurance and named Hazel Clews as the sole beneficiary. It's obvious he knew her and knew her well.'

'He never went out with another woman.'

'Then how did he spend all the time he was away from the farm?'

'He would never have betrayed our marriage.' Her voice trembled.

'Mrs Knott, did you murder your husband?'

'No,' she cried.

'Then give us the facts because they can't harm you. But if you go on lying . . .'

She interrupted him. 'I've told you the truth.'

'Mrs Knott, you knew your husband was having an affair with a woman almost half his age. You went to Trighton to identify this woman. She says you looked mad with jealousy.'

'She's lying. I tell you, she's lying.'

'If you did leave this place on Monday, the gardener will almost certainly know. When I leave here, I'm going to question him.'

'He'll swear I never left.' She began to sob, deep, shuddering sobs that shook her whole body. Tears streamed down her cheeks. 'Daniel never went out with another woman : he couldn't have betrayed me.'

Clayton sighed. He led the way out of the room and across the hall. As they left the cover of the porch heavy spatters of rain fell on them and as they sat down in the car the rain began to drum on the roof with an ever-increasing intensity until it was virtually a cloudburst.

Clayton leaned back in his seat. 'Not a bad evening's work,' he said bitterly. 'Two women reduced to tears.'

'God, what women!' said Burrows.

What women, thought Clayton, yet that did not prevent their suffering. Sometimes, police work made him think that living and suffering were the same thing and it was only when he returned to the warm comfort of his own home that he knew this to be nonsense.

Jarrold lived half a mile away in a road that was in sharp contrast with the one the detectives had just left. A council housing estate stretched its length and here there were no large gardens, no luxury flats, no architectural follies, only square boxes, differing from each other merely in small details.

They were able to park close to No. 14 and a short run through the driving rain brought them to an open porch which gave them some protection until their knock was answered.

Jarrold was a small, middle-aged man, barely five feet three in height, with a face that immediately reminded Clayton of a ferret because of its sharp inquisitiveness. His wife was a colourless woman, unattractive, and the moment she learned who they were it was clear she was worried. Jarrold appeared totally unworried and continued to watch the television to the end of the programme. As the credits came up, he switched it off and then looked at Clayton, a sly expression on his face.

'You know Mrs Knott, don't you?' said Clayton, as he sat down on the settee.

'I know 'er to look at,' said Jarrold.

'Then will you tell me whether Mrs Knott was at Miss Corrins's house last Monday?'

Jarrold brought a tin out of his pocket, opened it, and began to roll himself a cigarette. 'You want to know about last Monday?'

Clayton was watching Mrs Jarrold's face. He did not miss the signs of great nervousness, nor the way in which she kept looking at her husband in what was almost a pleading manner. He remembered how both Miss Corrins and Mrs Knott had been so insistent that Jarrold would swear Mrs Knott had never left the house.

'Mrs Knott was there Monday,' said Jarrold. He struck a match and lit his cigarette. 'That were the day Miss Corrins told me to dig out a new bed: I told 'er it was a stupid place for a new rose-bed, but she didn't never listen.'

'Can you say whether Mrs Knott left the house at any time during Monday?'

Jarrold shook his head. 'No, she didn't.'

'You're quite sure?'

'I wouldn't talk otherwise.'

'How d'you know she didn't go out?'

'I've got eyes, ain't I? The new rose-bed were in the front of the 'ouse.'

Clayton spoke pleasantly. 'We know you're lying.'

Mrs Jarrold drew in her breath with a sharp hiss. Her worry became fear.

'I'm tellin' you she never left the 'ouse.' Jarrold's voice rose.

'She was in Trighton at two in the afternoon.' Clayton's voice hardened. 'This is a murder case. People who set out to lie are going to end up in real trouble.'

Jarrold said nothing.

'Why are you lying? Did Miss Corrins bribe you to say that Mrs Knott never left the house?'

Jarrold threw the cigarette into the fireplace.

'Joe!' cried his wife.

'Belt up,' he muttered.

'Joe, tell 'em. It ain't right.'

'There ain't nothing to tell.'

Her voice grew shriller. 'I said you didn't ought to've took the money.'

'I ain't taken no money from no one.'

'You're forgetting something,' said Clayton. 'I told you, we can prove she was in Trighton on Monday afternoon so that makes you a liar from the start. Would you rather tell us the truth now and come to no harm, or will you go on lying and end up in court on a perjury charge that's good for several years in prison?'

Mrs Jarrold put her hand to her mouth in a gesture of anguish. 'Tell 'em,' she cried, for the second time.

Jarrold slowly rolled himself a second cigarette and his ferret-like face was filled with indecision. He lit the cigarette. 'She give me ten pound,' he said suddenly, 'for sayin' Mrs Knott never left the 'ouse.'

'I said it weren't right to take the money,' his wife said.

Jarrold spoke with fierce contempt. 'All you said was that I ought to have took the old bitch for twice as much.'

'That ain't true . . .'

'When in fact did Mrs Knott leave?' asked Clayton, hastily interrupting what appeared to be the beginning of a family row.

'She drove away in Miss Corrins's car just after I'd finished me grub.'

'Which makes it what time?'

'Near enough half one.'

'What sort of state d'you reckon she was in?'

'Wild,' he answered simply.

'How d'you mean?'

'She looked like crazy and drove out of the place so fast she near crashed with a bus. The old woman'd come out and shouted at 'er, but she didn't 'ear nothing.'

'Do you know what time she returned?'

Jarrold scratched his pointed nose. 'It weren't more'n a few minutes afore I stopped work.'

'And when did you stop?'

'Four-thirty.'

'Did you see her at this time?'

'Not me—just 'eard the car. I was round the back, in the green'ouse.'

'Then how do you know it was her?'

He seemed puzzled by the question. 'It couldn't 'ave been no one else. Miss Corrins's car was back in the drive when I cycled away.'

Clayton stood up.

'Mister—what about the ten quid she gave me?' asked Jarrold.

'I'd strongly advise handing it back.' Clayton did not imagine that his advice would be heeded.

Clayton arrived home at nine forty-five and in next to no time he was sitting down in the sitting-room.

'How did it go, love?' asked Margery.

'Lousy.'

'Has something gone wrong, then?'

'Not really wrong, but I've had to spend the evening proving to their face that two women were liars and it's not a happy sort of thing to do.'

She sat down on the arm of his chair. 'You're looking tireder than ever. It's a good thing we're off on a holiday soon.'

He spoke slowly. 'Margery, if this case doesn't get cleared up soon . . .'

'It doesn't matter what does or doesn't get done, you're going and no argument. You need a holiday and a holiday you'll have.'

He didn't try to argue, only too happy to enjoy the

absolute certainty of her declaration. She put an arm round him and cradled his head against her side.

The telephone rang.

'Blast!' she snapped. 'That'll be Superintendent Barry. I meant to tell you, he's rung twice already this evening.'

He groaned and stood up. He went out into the hall and answered the call.

'Just wanted to say how pleased I am with the way this case has been handled, Jim. By the way, I had a word with Superintendent Akers and he said your local knowledge had come in quite handy. As I've always said, you can't beat the value of local knowledge. Have there been any recent developments?'

'Mrs Knott's alibi has now been broken,' said Clayton.

There was a long whistle. 'Has it, indeed! By God, you know, whatever you think you've got to hand it to these London boys—they don't miss a trick.'

'Only those which are trumped.'

'What's that?' snapped Barry.

'Nothing, sir.'

'Sometimes, I don't understand a word you say . . . So the case is over and done with, bar the shouting. Nice work, Jim. It looks good in the records, clearing up a case as tricky as this. I'm glad you've been able to be of some assistance.'

CHAPTER XVI

MONDAY WAS an overcast day, but the storms had died away and the earth had the clean, renewed look that came when rain followed a long, dry period. The wind had swung round to the north-east and there was a chill to it, as if giving the first warnings of the coming winter.

When Clayton read the report from the county forensic

laboratory he learned that the shot recovered from Knott's body was size 3.

He began to tap on the desk with his fingers. Size 3 shot was too large for the ordinary game or vermin shooting that Knott would have done. He recalled the details of his search of the gun-room at Knott Farm. On top of the gun cupboard had been a cardboard case of cartridges containing eight boxes. One of the boxes had been green, the others a browny red. There had been no significance in this at the time, but was there any now in the light of the size of shot which had killed Knott?

Bodmin came into the room with some papers which he put on Akers's desk.

'Is Superintendent Akers around?' asked Clayton.

'He's gone out to collect the handwritten letters Alexander was supposed to have left behind : he's going to have them checked against Hazel Clews's handwriting, sir. He's also going to see if Knott's writing can be identified on the business correspondence.' Bodmin had a voice almost totally devoid of inflection.

'Tell him when you see him I've gone out to the farm, will you? After that, I'll be seeing Hulton's ex-boss.'

'Yes, sir.'

Clayton left and went down to his car.

Signs of change were already apparent at Knott Farm. The tumbledown post-and-rail fencing along the drive had been pulled out and a three-stranded barbed-wire fence had been erected in its place, the thistles in the right-hand small paddock had been slashed, and across the road the gate into the paddocks had been re-hung.

The Bentley was not in the garage and when he knocked on the front door of the house—which started the dogs barking—there was no answer. He waited, knocked again, and then found the key, opened the door, and went inside.

The house was, in sharp contrast with his previous visit,

dirty and in disorder. In the kitchen, used cutlery was stacked higgledy-piggledy on the draining board and on the table was a plate on which was some bacon that was growing mould.

The gun-room was exactly as it had been before. He took the cardboard case down from the top of the gun cupboard and opened up the flaps. The boxes were as he remembered them : seven were a light browny red and contained number 5 shot, the eighth was green and contained cartridges of 3 shot. In this eighth box there were only two cartridges out of the original five of the top row. Why were there three missing and not two, he wondered, a perplexed frown on his forehead? He carried the case out of the house, locked up, replaced the key, and put the case in the boot of the car.

He walked up the drive to the farm buildings and, hearing the thumping beat of a tractor, continued round to the concrete float. Hulton was using the foreloader to clean out last year's dung from one of the bays. Clayton waited until the bucket was emptied into an old tipping trailer, then shouted at the top of his voice : 'Can I have a word with you?'

Hulton's expression was angry. 'What's it this time?'

'I shan't keep you for long.'

Hulton pulled out the stop button and the engine clattered to a stop, causing the tractor to vibrate heavily.

'That sounds even worse than last time,' said Clayton, nodding at the tractor.

'It's like everything else on the farm, totally neglected. The oil level was hardly showing on the dipstick, the oil seals in the rams were perished . . .' He drew the back of his hand across his forehead, leaving behind a smear of dirt. 'How could any man treat property like this?' He scrambled over the hydraulic pipes and the foreloader arm and jumped to the ground. 'Well, what d'you want this time? Why the hell can't you blokes leave me alone to get on with the work—it's not as though there's nothing to do. And, god-damn it, I've only just got rid of one smooth-tongued, oily bastard.'

That, decided Clayton, was a pleasing description of Akers. 'I'm sorry, but we've a job to do, same as you.'

Hulton noisily cleared his throat, then spat. 'My job's of some use.' He leaned against the back wheel of the tractor, careless of all the dung on it.

'You know Daniel Knott was murdered while he was carrying out an insurance swindle?'

'So the other bloke told me. Trust the old fool to make a hash of even that.'

'You don't seem very surprised he was on a swindle?'

'If you'd ever met him, you wouldn't be surprised by any goddamn twisted thing he did.'

'Had you some idea of what was going on?'

'No.'

'This farm's worth thirty-five thousand quid, forgetting all the woods. That's a lot of money,' said Clayton.

'In the state it's in now, you'd have to be a bloody fool to pay that sort of money for it,' retorted Hulton. 'Anyway, it's unkind land. This yellow clay is death to good farm-ing.'

'Yet you were keen enough to get here to farm it.'

'What d'you expect? It's mine. If it was a desert, I'd've rushed to farm it. Christ, man, can't you understand how I'd rather farm this place when I own it than make twice as much for half the work as the manager of the finest Fen farm in the country? It's mine. It's my land.' He stared out past the exterior Dutch barn at the lie-back field in which were the cows. Just for a moment, there was the look of a visionary in his heavy, almost sullen face.

Clayton spoke. 'Let's talk about last Monday.'

'Again?'

'What time did you start work in the afternoon?'

'One-thirty.'

'And you worked until when?'

'It was time to break off and milk the cows.'

'When did Fingle come out to the field you were cutting?'

'I've gone through all this before.'

'Go through it again.'

Hulton brought a packet of cigarettes out of his pocket. After a moment's hesitation, he offered it, then lit a match for them both. 'He was out early on, then he was around again at three-thirty, shouting at me for stopping cutting. Like I said to him, "You milk the cows and I'll keep cutting." That shut the old bastard up.'

'Where's the nearest telephone to the field you were working in?'

'What's that?' he asked, for the first time showing any emotion other than sullen resentment.

Clayton repeated the question.

Hulton's brow creased in thought. 'There's a call-box at the cross-roads in the village.'

'How long d'you reckon it would take to walk from the field you were in to the call-box?'

'Five minutes.'

'Did you make a call from there last Monday afternoon?'

'Of course not. Why the hell should I've done?'

'Someone may have telephoned Mrs Knott at around half-past one to tell her where she could find her husband's girl-friend.'

'Why bother to do that?'

'In order to cause mischief: so much mischief that Mrs Knott became wild with grief and rage.'

Hulton jerked himself upright and then climbed back on to the seat of the tractor. 'I didn't phone her, or anyone else.' He started the tractor and worked the hand throttle until the noise of the engine was too loud for any further conversation.

Clayton returned to his car. He backed down to the road,

noted the time, and then drove cross-country to Idenford and Jacktree Farm. The journey, thanks to all the narrow, winding lanes and blind corners, took him sixty-five minutes.

Fingle was bowed right over by rheumatism and he not only had to use a stick to walk, but also had to hold his head up at a painful angle to see where he was going.

He cursed Hulton for a thankless no-good who'd returned endless kindnesses by quitting his job without notice and leaving Fingle in a terrible state with cows to milk, hay to turn . . . Clayton brought the conversation round to the question of confirming Hulton's evidence. Fingle had gone down to the five-acre field at a quarter past two to see if the grass was being cut properly and he had returned there at three-thirty to find Hulton had stopped because, he claimed, it was time to get the cows in and milk them. Hulton, being stupid, incompetent, and pig-headed, had always insisted on milking at the same time when everyone knew that it didn't matter if the milking was an hour or two late because hay was being made . . .

Clayton thanked the other and left. He again timed himself on the journey back to Knott Farm and drove as fast as he dared. After scaring himself twice, he arrived within fifty-five minutes. No one could do the journey in less than forty-five minutes, so that it was quite impossible that Hulton could have been at Knott Farm at five past three that Monday afternoon.

On his return to the police station, Clayton went up to the CID general room. DC Pritchard was there, trying to type out a report and becoming infuriated as his fingers hit either the wrong keys or else several all together so that everything jammed.

Clayton handed Pritchard the cardboard case of cartridges. 'Take these to Dabs at HQ. See the detective-sergeant and ask him to check each box for prints and also each of the cartridges inside the boxes. On the way, take a

K

couple of clean mug shots to the Corrins woman's place and hand them to Mrs Knott—who's bound to be there—and ask her if she recognizes them. Give the photos to Dabs for comparison prints.'

'Right, sir.' Pritchard stood up, obviously very happy to leave the typewriter.

'You may . . .' Clayton stopped. It seemed unnecessary to warn against the kind of reception Miss Corrins would probably offer. Pritchard's ebullient character was surely proof against her, even in her most virulent form.

Clayton walked along to his own room, which thankfully proved to be empty. He sat down and checked through the yellow pages of the telephone directory for the list of gunsmiths. There were two in Gertfinden, two in Parqueton, and one in Relstone. He knew Janes and Lincs to be the bigger of the two in town and he telephoned them and asked to speak to the manager.

'Mr Knott?' said the manager. 'Yes, he always comes to us. When he first moved down here, he bought a gun—a very nice sidelock Churchill, I seem to remember.'

'Did he buy cartridges from you?'

'We supplied him with a considerable number when he had his own shoot, but I understand he gave that up, due to cost—although obviously things weren't as they should be. I did hear . . .' There was a short cough. 'I was told you could always buy a brace of pheasants in the village.'

'Have you sold him cartridges recently?'

'I couldn't say off-hand, but he always bought on account so I could find out from the records.'

'Will you have a check for me, then? If he did buy some, will you also find out if possible what make they were and what size shot?'

'I'll ring you back, shall I?'

Clayton telephoned the other gunsmiths. None of them had ever knowingly dealt with Knott.

The manager of Janes and Lincs reported back after twenty minutes. 'We last sold a case of two hundred and fifty cartridges to Mr Knott in April. They were Eley Grand Prix, number five shot. The assistant remembers Mr Knott saying he was doing no more than wander round his own woods rough shooting and wanted the best all-round shot size.'

'That's fine. And you haven't sold any single boxes to him at any time?'

'I can't guarantee that, of course. He could have paid cash and one of the young assistants either didn't know him or couldn't remember him.'

'Do you stock Super County size three shot cartridges?'

'No, we don't.'

'Many thanks for all your help. I'll send someone round later on for a written statement.' Clayton rang off. He stared unseeingly at the far wall.

DC Pritchard returned to the station at seven-fifteen that night. He exchanged ribald comments with a uniformed constable in the corridor, then playfully made a football tackle—his sixteen stone sent the other flying into the wall with a hard thump. The PC swore his shoulder was broken and Pritchard roared with laughter.

He reported to Clayton and put the case of cartridges on the desk. 'Dabs has carried out all the tests, sir. Mrs Knott's prints are on the box of Super County cartridges, but not on any of the others.'

'Are there any other prints?'

'None on any of the boxes.'

'What about the cartridges?'

'Two of the cartridges from the Super County box had her dabs on 'em, but all others were clear.'

'Did they take photos?'

'Yes, sir. You'll get a set with the typed report.'

'Good. Thanks.'

The senior legal assistant from the Director of Public Prosecution's office—advising because this was a murder case—
leafed through the papers he had taken from his brief-case.
He was a middle-aged man, with a cheerful round face that
held a hint of authority. He wore thick horn-rimmed
glasses. 'It's a case which relies very heavily on circumstantial evidence,' he said.

'Quite so, sir,' said Akers, 'but murder cases usually do.'

'I am aware of that fact,' replied the other drily. 'What
I'm saying is that this case relies more than usual on such
evidence.'

Akers, thought Clayton, was unaware of the implied
rebuke. Could any words pierce that armour-plated self-
confidence?

Akers leaned forward. 'There are three possible bene-
ficiaries to the murder and four possible suspects, Clews and
Shear, Mrs Knott, and Hulton. Clews, Shear, and Hulton
all have alibis for the time of death, Mrs Knott does not. A
jury has to be really stupid to miss the significance of that
evidence.'

'We must not overlook the fact that the time of death is to
a large extent an assumption. There is no proof that the
shot fired at five past three killed Knott . . .'

Akers interrupted him. 'No actual proof, maybe, but
overwhelming circumstantial evidence. Knott drove up to
the farm at two-fifteen in the van. We know for fact that
there was no shot fired between two-fifteen and three-five.

'What we know is that no shot was heard.' The legal
assistant took off his spectacles, polished them with his handkerchief, then replaced them. 'Still, the defence will not press
this point since they've little to gain from doing so.' He
turned over a sheet of paper. 'I'm not too happy that we
have sufficient proof Knott was planning an insurance

fraud.' Seeing Akers was about to speak, he held up his hand. 'I'm not disputing the attempted fraud, I'm merely saying that a rather complicated set of facts has to be explained in terms that the jury will readily understand. If possible, I'd like some evidence of his intended actions after the time of his faked death which will demonstrate a total break in habit that can allow of only one explanation.' He leaned back in his chair. 'When a man intends this sort of fraud, one of his main problems is to make certain he's not recognized anywhere after the time of his supposed death. What steps do you imagine Knott would have decided to take to avoid such recognition?'

'Since he lived so close to the coast, sir,' said Akers, 'it's a hundred to one he'd have gone abroad on a false passport. Then he'd have stayed abroad for good or for sufficiently long that on his return to this country he'd have been reasonably safe if he lived elsewhere.'

The senior legal assistant spoke to Clayton. 'Do you agree with that, Inspector?'

Clayton was amused by the expression on Akers's face—what need was there to seek confirmation from a mere DI? 'Yes, sir. I'd only add that I don't think he'd have gone far from the Channel ports because he'd have wanted to see both his forty thousand pounds and girl-friend as soon as possible.'

'Quite. Which is why it will be worth asking assistance from the French, Dutch, and Belgian police to try to discover whether a longish reservation which was not taken up was made at a coastal hotel for the night of the twenty-first of this month. If the reservation was made by letter, the letter might even have been kept.'

'It's a bit of a long-shot,' said Akers.

'Nevertheless, I want that done. And while we're talking about letters, have you been able to identify the writers of the correspondence found in "Alexander's room?"'

'The handwriting experts say the letters signed Alice were not written by Hazel Clews. On the other hand, they're ready to testify the official correspondence in Alexander's name was, when handwritten, written by Knott.'

The senior legal assistant pursed his lips. 'We're no nearer, then, to proving Hazel Clews knew of the intended fraud?'

'No, sir, but surely when she's in the witness-box counsel will be able to force an admission?'

'Perhaps you're overlooking something? The prosecution will be calling Miss Clews. If in her evidence-in-chief she denies all knowledge of the fraud, she cannot be challenged on this denial unless there are grounds for having her declared a hostile witness.'

'I've always said the laws of evidence are bloody daft,' muttered Akers.

The French police reported by teleprinter on Saturday, September 2. A reservation by post had been made by an Englishman, Fergusson, at the Hotel Corniche in Rue d'Alsace, Calais: Fergusson had booked a double room with bathroom for three weeks, starting August 21st, and had said his wife would be joining him later. He had never turned up. His letter of reservation was on the files.

At the preliminary hearing before the magistrates an application was made to dismiss the case on the grounds of insufficient evidence. The application was rejected. The defence was reserved and Mrs Phyllis Knott was sent for trial at the next Assize.

The Claytons went on their holiday to Jersey.

CHAPTER XVII

THE JUDGE scratched his head under his wig with the cap of the ball-point pen he was using. He was a lean-faced man with a seemingly haughty expression of disdain, as if the happenings of mere mortals were of little account : it was a false impression because he was a man of considerable compassion who was always more concerned with justice than with the strict letter of the law. He asked the pathologist to repeat what he had just said, made a note in his book, then spoke to the jury and asked them if they fully understood the significance of what they had just heard. The foreman of the jury stood up. 'I . . . I think so, my Lord,' he answered.

The judge addressed prosecuting counsel. 'Mr Riger, will you please go through this evidence again? It is very important that the jury are absolutely clear about what they have been told.'

'Yes, my Lord.' Riger was a large man, some called him gross, with a naturally long face that was elongated by his double chin. He turned to face the witness-box. 'Will a body be preserved by keeping it at low temperature?'

The pathologist was plainly annoyed at having to repeat his evidence. 'A body is preserved and the colder the atmosphere, the better the state of preservation. Zero, Fahrenheit, is not in this respect particularly cold but ordinary food can be kept in domestic freezer cabinets for a number of months : indeed, people have kept food under these conditions for years and eaten it without any noticeable ill-effect.'

'Have you from your own experience knowledge of the possibilities of preserving a human body in cold storage?'

'Not beyond the short storage which is carried out in morgues.'

'Do you, as an expert witness, have knowledge obtained from other sources concerning the possibilities of such storage?'

'Yes.'

'Will you please tell the court what you know?'

'The human body can be preserved in cold storage in the same way that other once-living tissues can be. To exclude initial decay it's necessary to freeze the whole body as soon as possible and this is difficult in an ordinary domestic freezer. However, if the freezer has an over-riding control it can be set to work continuously beforehand so that the temperature is lowered well below zero, in which case the extra degree of cold will help to cool down to zero an average-sized body without much initial decay.

'At zero degrees, or thereabouts, a body is rigid and solid : perhaps the best comparison is with a block of ice. It is in a state of preservation, although at this temperature it will not stay preserved for ever.'

'Would you expect much change within six months?' asked counsel.

'I don't think so, but I know of no research into that question.'

'Thank you. Will you now please deal with the relevant aspects of thawing out?'

'A human body thaws out like any other substance, but being a large thing it takes a considerable time at ordinary room temperatures. Once thawed, decay will set in and there is some authority for saying that the rate of decay will be faster than it would have been had the body not been frozen.'

'Can you tell from a physical examination whether a body has been subjected to freezing?'

'Freezing causes no changes in itself. If, however, one suspects freezing took place, then some loss of detail of body cell structure may be apparent on microscopic examination. I should,' he said pugnaciously, 'like to make it quite clear that this loss of detail will almost certainly be missed unless the investigator is warned on the possibility that the body underwent freezing.'

'Were you so warned?'

'I was not.'

'Would the damage caused by the fire have had any effect on your ability to discover evidence of freezing, had you been warned of the possibility?'

'It was so severe that no evidence of freezing could have survived.'

Riger looked at the judge, who nodded. 'Will you now please tell the court the results of the post-mortem,' said Riger.

The pathologist gave his evidence, rarely pausing to check his evidence.

Browland had dressed with great care, yet this fact was certainly not apparent to anyone in court who saw him for the first time : coat and trousers came from different suits, his shirt had a tear just below the collar, which was much too loose, and his tie was badly stained. Strangely, when in the witness-box he was initially far less nervous than normal and did not fiddle with his nose. He gave his evidence coherently, only occasionally finding difficulty in answering.

Hapwood, QC, rose to cross-examine. He was a small man, with a face seemingly set at the oddest angles. He had a mellifluous voice and a love of the rolling phrase. He had been called to the Bar at a time when influence initially counted for far more than ability, yet he, without knowing a single solicitor who could feed him with work, had become a successful junior within seven years and had taken silk after twenty. 'I'd like to know a little more about this shot-gun in the store-room. Did you ever handle it?'

'No,' replied Browland.

'Have you, in fact, ever fired a gun?'

'I ain't, never.' Browland suddenly looked apprehensive,

very worried that the questioning was about to turn to the subject of pheasants.

'You cannot tell us what kind of a gun it was?'

'It were a double 'ammer.'

'Was it a twelve-bore?'

'It were that.'

'How do you know this?'

'Mr Knott put 'is ordinary cartridges in it.'

'Did he use this gun much?'

'It were only for vermin.'

'Would you say it was in good condition?'

'It were rusty, but Mr Knott 'ad it checked to see it were safe to fire.'

'And did it always hang on the wall above the tank containing diesel fuel?'

'That's right.'

'Was it there on the Monday?'

'I dunno.'

'When had you last seen it?'

Browland became uneasy.

The judge spoke in a friendly voice. 'If you don't know, just say so. There is nothing wrong in not knowing.'

'I dunno, sir.'

'Did you go into that store-room on the Monday?' asked Hapwood.

'I dunno.'

Hapwood turned and said something to his junior, then faced the witness-box once more. 'Am I correct in saying that in so far as you do know, that gun could have been missing from its usual place for several days?'

'I dunno.'

Hapwood shrugged his shoulders in a quick gesture of irritation, but the tenor of his voice had not changed when he next spoke. 'How much diesel oil was in the tank?'

'It were about 'alf full, I think.'

'And how much paraffin was in the drum?'

'I dunno.'

'Did either container leak?'

'The pump on the diesel leaked a bit. Then there was always some dripped out when the 'ose was brought back in.'

'So presumably all this spilled over the floor?'

'The floor were always in a mess.'

'Was there usually much rubbish lying around—paper sacks, ordinary sacks, rags, that sort of thing?'

'Mr Knott was always on at me to clear it up, but 'e paid me to milk the cows, not for nothing more.'

'And you did not clean up?'

' ' E paid me to . . .'

'Quite so. Was there much else in the store-room that was inflammable?'

'Doing what?' asked Browland, bewildered by the question.

'Were there many other things that would burn easily?'

'There were bits of wood and things.'

'Let us now deal with the early afternoon of Monday, the twenty-first of August. You were at your home, which is near Cregiton cross-roads?'

'That's right.'

'And after lunch you went out?'

Browland suddenly fiddled with his nose. 'I wanted to go for a walk.' He looked nervously at Hapwood.

'And while you were out on this walk you heard a shot?'

'Yes.'

'You told my learned friend that what you heard was both barrels of the shot-gun from the store-room being fired simultaneously. How do you know the gun used was the one from the store-room?'

Browland wriggled his shoulders. 'The police said it were that gun,' he mumbled.

Hapwood stared at the jury, an expression of surprise on his face. 'Do you mean that you're giving us the police's evidence, not your own?'

'I . . . I 'eard that shot.'

'You heard a shot. But isn't it fact that you have little idea what gun fired it?'

Browland stared dumbly at Hapwood.

'You said the shot came from the direction of the farm. Are you quite certain of that?'

'Yes.'

'Would you not agree that woods often distort the direction of a sound?'

'It seemed to come from there.'

' "Seemed to". You're suddenly very much less certain than you were.'

'I dunno,' said Browland desperately.

'Tell me, can you even be certain you did not hear any other shots that afternoon?'

'There weren't none others.'

'Or you just didn't hear any others?'

'There weren't none others,' he cried.

Hapwood was about to continue that line of attack when he checked himself. Experience told him that to continue would be merely to alienate the jury, no matter how muddled he made the witness appear. 'Did you have much to do with the general running of the farm?'

'I only did the milking—'e didn't pay me for doing nothing more.'

'So although you've told us the condition of the farm was going from bad to worse, you can't know this from your own observations?'

'But it were terrible. The milk kept dropping and what's more the cows wouldn't come bulling, they was thick with mastitis, and them what was calving was retaining their cleansings.'

Hapwood leaned back and spoke to his junior. 'What the hell's he talking about, Gerald?'

'Search me. It's obviously a lot easier to get your milk straight from the bottle.'

Hapwood turned over another page of the transcript of Browland's evidence before the magistrates. He had, as always, made notes for his cross-examination in the margins and, as always, he had great difficulty in reading these notes. He began to question Browland about the fire.

The assize courtroom was part of the ugly, bombastic town hall in Relstone. The nearest police station with a canteen was a mile away and therefore Clayton lunched at a pub. He had eaten half his sandwiches when he saw Akers come into the bar. He silently groaned.

Akers ordered a half-pint of bitter and came across to Clayton's table and sat down. 'Everything's going very smoothly,' he said with satisfaction.

'It certainly seems to be, sir.'

'The press benches are full, aren't they? As a matter of fact, I had quite a job to get away from the photographers just now.' Akers drank, then put his glass on the table. 'Those sandwiches look all right,' he remarked.

Clayton pushed the plate across.

'That's noble of you,' said Akers. He ate a sandwich. 'The ham's a bit stale.' He picked up a second sandwich and ate that. 'Well—how's life in the sticks?'

'Pretty much as it's always been.'

'Plenty of cases of chicken-stealing to keep you busy?' Akers smiled. He took a handkerchief from the pocket of the very smart grey pin-striped suit he was wearing and brushed some crumbs away from his lips. 'I've had one or two quite interesting cases since I was down here . . . Don't mind if I have that last sandwich, do you? . . . but I managed to clear them up fairly smartly. You probably read about the one in Oxford.'

'No, I didn't.'

'You didn't?' Akers was very surprised.

Clayton finished his beer and put the glass down on the table in such a way that Akers could not help but notice it was empty. Akers did notice, but failed to do anything about it.

Hazel Clews went into the witness-box at three o'clock in the afternoon, just as the lights were turned on because the heavily overcast sky had made the courtroom quite gloomy.

She had dressed and made up with a far more conservative taste than usual and although nothing could hide her essential sexuality, there was at least an air of some propriety to it.

Her evidence-in-chief was fairly brief. She admitted she and Knott had had an affair, but said that Knott had made all the running and had told her his marriage had completely broken down. Because of this, she'd never felt she was harming his wife. Mrs Knott, who until that moment had sat huddled in the dock, suddenly stood up and shouted that Hazel Clews was a liar and she'd never had an affair with her husband. The burly wardress ordered Mrs Knott to be quiet and Hapwood whispered instructions to his junior, who left his seat, went down the steps to the dock, and spoke briefly to her.

Hapwood cross-examined. 'Were you madly in love with Daniel Knott, a man almost twice your age?' he asked quietly.

'Of course not,' she snapped.

'Then in so far as you were concerned, this was just a casual affair?'

Too late, she realized how with one question he had stripped away most of her pretence.

'How soon after you met did you first have sexual intercourse with him? One day, two days?'

'It wasn't like that,' she said loudly.

'What was it like, then?'

She did not answer.

'Miss Clews, we have heard that Daniel Knott took out a life insurance for forty thousand pounds in March and named you sole beneficiary. When did you first know about this?'

'I said I never did.'

'I did hear you make that denial to my learned friend, but I thought perhaps you might now wish to reconsider your answer.'

'Why should I?'

'One good reason might be that you're on oath to tell the truth.'

'That is the truth.'

'We shall have to examine the matter more closely. When and how did you first meet Daniel Knott?'

'In October last year. He came into the shop and bought some flowers.'

'Was this in the beginning of the month?'

'It was about the middle.'

'When did you first have sexual intercourse with him?'

'I can't remember.'

Hapwood picked up a piece of paper. 'I have a certified bank statement here . . . Usher, pass copies to his lordship and the jury, please . . . and it shows that in the last week of October, Daniel Knott started drawing cash cheques on a hitherto unprecedented scale. It seems reasonable to suppose that most of this extra money was spent on you.'

'He didn't take me out much,' she protested sullenly.

'By February, Daniel Knott had an overdraft of twelve hundred pounds and the bank was pressing for repayment. From then on, the amount drawn was of necessity far smaller and as a direct result he could not spend nearly as much on you. I suggest that this led to great discontent on your part?'

'That's a lie.'

'I suggest you went out with him because you originally

thought he was very much better off than he was and that when you discovered the truth you threatened to have nothing more to do with him?'

'No.'

'Which is why, besotted in his love for you, he set out to conduct an insurance swindle. I further suggest that in order to hold your interest he told you all about the swindle and the forty thousand pounds?'

The judge intervened. 'Mr Hapwood, by your questions you have inferred the existence of a number of facts—that Knott spent a great deal of money on entertaining this witness, that this witness believed him to be rich, that when she discovered he was not she threatened to break off her relationship with him, and that she was fully aware of the intended insurance swindle. What proof have you of these allegations?'

'My Lord, it is obvious from the surrounding facts and the nature of the friendship so clearly outlined by the witness herself at the start of the cross-examination . . .'

'I will not, Mr Hapwood, have counsel inferring matters of a derogatory nature when there is no proof to support such inferences.'

Hapwood, slightly surprised he had been allowed to continue for as long as he had, was satisfied that he had persuaded the jury this witness was not as blameless as she had managed to suggest in her examination-in-chief.

The judge addressed the jury. 'Members of the jury, you will be very careful to distinguish between proven facts, proved on evidence given in this court, and allegations made by counsel.'

Hapwood remained unworried. Nothing the judge could say would now alter the picture in the jury's minds of a man going out with a woman half his age, spending a great deal of money on her, and then when the bank refused to lend him any more, turning to an insurance fraud because he longed for the woman beyond any other consideration. 'Miss Clews, on Monday, the twenty-first of August, you claim to have seen a woman outside the shop where you worked. You identified her as Mrs Knott. How many times previously had you seen Mrs Knott?'

'Once.'

'That refers, does it, to the time you and Daniel Knott were dining at a restaurant and she surprised you both?'

'She didn't surprise me,' snapped Hazel Clews.

'Then you expected to meet her there?'

'That's not what I meant.'

'Please tell us what you did mean?' said Hapwood mockingly.

'What I meant was . . . We were doing nothing but having a meal.'

'What else could you have been doing?'

'You've got a dirty mind,' she snapped.

There was considerable laughter and it was several seconds before the usher's calls for silence were heeded.

Hapwood smiled, as if relishing the jest against himself, but those who knew him well could judge how false that smile was. 'You were very vague about when and where this meeting took place: you suggested it might have been in April. That puts it at roughly four months before August the twenty-first?'

'Well?'

'And you did not see Mrs Knott between then and the moment when you claim to have seen her outside the shop where you work?'

'No.'

'You have also stated that her features were distorted by emotion—you compared her to a woman having a fit. The features of a person under great emotional stress become considerably changed, don't they?'

'It was her.'

L

'But you hadn't seen her for four months . . .'

'I tell you, it was her. She'd come to find out who I was.'

'How d'you know that?'

'Ain't it obvious?'

'So on top of the weakest of identifications, you are adding a supposition for which you have no proof?'

Hazel Clews made no answer.

Hapwood leaned back against the front of his junior's desk. There was no point in pursuing the matter further— it was quite certain Mrs Knott had not been at Miss Corrins's at two that afternoon.

It was a hell of a case, he reflected. The murder had been committed for gain, three people stood to gain from the death, four people might have carried out the shooting, yet all except Mrs Knottt had alibis. Defence counsel was not offered a sporting chance.

CHAPTER XVIII

THE ALARM woke up Clayton. He reached out for the clock to turn off the alarm, but only succeeded in knocking it to the floor with a loud clatter. Margery woke up. 'Sorry,' he said.

She yawned. 'I'll bet you did that on purpose!'

'Certainly not,' he protested.

'You can't bear to think anyone else is asleep when you're awake : it's the sadistic streak in you.'

He pulled back the bedclothes.

'Don't get out on your side,' she said urgently.

'Why ever not?'

'It's Friday the thirteenth so you know you mustn't get out on the right-hand side of the bed.'

'You and your superstitions,' he said jeeringly.

'All right, be pig-headed and get out on your side. And

when the house burns down, everything goes wrong for you in court today, and Superintendent Akers is detailed back here for a much longer case, just remember what I said.'

He could ignore the threat of fire, or something going wrong in court, but the thought of Akers decided him. He carefully began to climb over her. She tickled him and he collapsed on top of her.

'You're just as superstitious as me,' she said, 'but you try to be all he-man tough and hide it.'

He kissed her, then scrambled down on to the floor.

'What time will you be back, Jim?' she asked.

'God knows! I'm getting to the office early to cope with some of my other work before I move to Relstone, but I'll have to return to the station afterwards.'

'Will the trial finish today?'

'Not a chance.'

'How's Mrs Knott taking it?'

He spoke slowly. 'She looks utterly beaten.'

'It must be terrible to have to live with something you did in a moment of passion.'

'I suppose so.'

She looked at him. 'Is something wrong, Jim?'

He shook his head. 'Just thinking.'

Cynics who knew Hapwood claimed that one could always judge how well his case was going by the degree to which he attacked the police witnesses : if he suggested that even their evidence as to name and rank was suspect, his case was a real floperoo.

'But who was in the house at that time?' he said belligerently, in the middle of his cross-examination of Clayton.

'No one, sir,' answered Clayton.

'Do you mean to tell us you broke into this house?' His voice rose.

'No, sir.'

'Not? But what else were you doing?'

'Mrs Knott had told me where the key was.'

'On this occasion or on a previous one?'

'On a previous one, sir, but she told me to go over the house when I wanted and so I assumed it would be all right on this second occasion.'

Hapwood stared up at the domed ceiling of the court-room. 'It is a terrible thing,' he said in solemn tones, 'to know that a policeman is likely to break into one's house whenever it is empty.' He lowered his gaze. 'Why did you not seek the owner's permission to enter?'

'I've already said what happened, sir. In any case, I wasn't quite certain who was the owner. If the farm was entailed to Mr Hulton, was Mr Hulton the owner right away or was Mrs Knott the owner until probate was granted?'

'That is sheer prevarication, aimed at keeping the court's attention away from what actually happened.'

The judge spoke. 'It is not unknown for counsel to pursue such tactics, Mr Hapwood.'

'Perhaps, my Lord, but no counsel would engage in such doubtful tactics before your lordship, whose dislike of such things is well known,' replied Hapwood blandly.

'Well known, but not always respected.'

Hapwood faced the witness-box again. 'You broke into this house and went through to the gun-room. Who was with you?'

'No one.'

'So there is no one who can verify your evidence?'

'No, sir, not on this point.'

'Wouldn't it have been very much better had there been someone?'

'Possibly, sir, but I had no men available—they were all too busy to accompany me on what could so easily have been a wasted journey.'

'But you made certain it wasn't wasted.'

'I merely checked the case of cartridges I had previously seen in the gun-room.'

'To see if there was one box inside of a different colour and of a different-sized shot to the others?'

'Yes, sir.'

'Since you had previously seen a box of a different colour, you must have known it was likely still to be there. I repeat, do you not think it would have been better to have had a witness?'

The judge intervened again. 'Mr Hapwood, are you accusing the witness of having lied about the manner of finding this case of cartridges and the number and type of boxes within it?'

'No, my Lord. I merely wish to establish all the facts and to point out that when important evidence is uncovered it is naturally better if two persons are present at the time rather than one.'

'Since you are satisfied the witness is telling the truth, this point becomes immaterial.'

Hapwood's shoulders slumped and his attitude suggested that his client was battling not only the prosecution but also a heavily biased judge. 'Did you examine the boxes of cartridges?' he finally asked.

'Only visually.'

'Were they neatly packed?'

'Yes, sir.'

'Was there anything to suggest when the green box had been put in the cardboard case?'

'No, sir.'

'So it could have been there for weeks?'

'Yes.'

'And in consequence might have nothing to do with this case?'

'That's possible.'

'And if my client says she put the box of Super County

cartridges in the case several weeks before the twenty-first of August, you cannot deny her evidence?'

'I have no proof to the contrary.'

Hapwood hitched up his gown. 'Inspector, you told my learned friend that you questioned all the gunsmiths and none of them had knowingly sold a box of Super County three shot cartridges to Mr Knott. Did you also question the staff of every shop which sells cartridges? Is it not a fact that some ironmongers sell cartridges? Do not sporting shops, which are not gunsmiths, sell cartridges?'

'Yes, sir. We questioned all known sources of cartridges in Gertfinden, Relstone, and Parqueton, without result.'

'But not the shops in Abbotsbridge?'

'No, sir.'

'Or Trighton?'

'No.'

'You don't seem to have made very great efforts, Inspector, to see whether Daniel Knott—contrary to all your theories—did in fact buy those cartridges.'

'We checked as far as we considered necessary, sir. We established the fact that Mr Knott had always bought all his cartridges from Janes and Lincs in Gertfinden. If he had bought this box of three shot, surely he would have had no cause to go anywhere else to try and hide his purchase?' And get round that one, thought Clayton.

Hapwood didn't get round the question—he just ignored it. 'Have you been able to prove that Mrs Knott bought this box of cartridges?'

'No, sir.'

'Can you prove there was not another box, or more than one, of the same make and kind of cartridge in the storeroom?'

'We were able to do no more than question Mr Browland on that point.'

'Which, no doubt, can only have led to confusion?'

'We didn't find him confused when we questioned him.'

'Perhaps,' said the judge, 'you do not have learned counsel's ability to confuse a witness.'

Hapwood bowed ironically at the Bench.

Hulton did not try to hide his feelings. 'Of course I hated seeing the farm go to rack and ruin.'

Hapwood flicked the tails of his wig away from his neck. 'Perhaps you saw it as your inheritance that was being squandered?'

'I saw it first as a farm.' Hulton thrust his square chin forward. 'It hurts to see any farm being ruined.'

'But must hurt far more when that farm will one day be yours?' Hapwood paused, then added: 'Should you, of course, live longer than the life tenant. You must often have wished something would happen to Daniel Knott so that you could take over the farm before it was too late? I suppose that from your point of view his death came at the very last moment?'

Hulton gripped his huge fists.

'How long had he been dead when you turned up at the farm to claim your inheritance?'

'Look, I came quickly . . .'

'So quickly your employer had no notice whatsoever you were going to leave his employment?'

'If you're so clever, tell me how a farm can run itself. Cows have got to be milked and fed. They don't live on empty words.'

'Unlike some counsel,' murmured Riger.

'Even with Daniel Knott dead, were there not the same number of persons about the farm as so often happened?' asked Hapwood smoothly.

Hulton hammered his fist on the side of the witness-box. 'I tell you, there wasn't anyone around who knew anything.'

'Mr Hulton, who's looking after the farm at this moment?'

'There's no one there right now . . .' Hulton's face reddened.

'So the farm can survive without you?' Hapwood paused for several seconds before continuing: 'You worked on a farm in the village of Idenford until you heard of the death of your uncle?'

'Yes.'

'How far by road is Idenford from Endley Cross?'

'Just on thirty miles.'

'How long does it normally take you to drive those thirty miles?'

'Near enough an hour.'

'What sort of car have you?'

'A small van.'

'Could the journey be done by a fast car in a lesser time—say three-quarters of an hour?'

'Maybe, if you aren't worried about the people.'

'If you had a really fast car, do you think the journey might be done in thirty minutes?'

'I haven't got a really fast car.'

'I said "if".'

'If I had a helicopter, I could fly.'

'Did you hire a helicopter to get from Jacktree Farm to Knott Farm?' asked Hapwood blandly.

'Of course I didn't.'

'Then we need waste no time on that supposition. Let me repeat the question: If you have a very powerful car and drove very fast, could you make the journey in thirty minutes?'

'No.'

'Thirty-five minutes?'

'I don't know. I haven't got a fast car. I don't drive fast.'

'Mr Fingle's watch would only have had to be a few minutes wrong to extend the possible time available to you for such a journey?'

Hulton's face flushed. 'I didn't kill Daniel.'

'But if you had been able to borrow a fast car, were an expert driver, and if Mr Fingle's watch was wrong by only a few minutes, the times show you could have done.'

'I didn't kill him,' he shouted.

Hapwood sat down.

Riger stood up. 'Are you quite certain you don't own a Ferrari or a Lamborghini?'

'Of course I am.'

'Have you any car other than your small Austin van?'

'No.'

'Did you, on or about the twenty-first of August, borrow or hire a very fast car?'

'No.'

'Are you an expert driver?'

'No.'

'Have you ever raced cars?'

'No.'

'Have you ever known anyone make this journey in forty-five minutes?'

'No.'

'Thank you, Mr Hulton.' As Hulton left the witness-box, his expression was one of frustrated anger.

'This would seem to have been a complicated case?' said Riger.

Akers, in the witness-box, nodded. 'Yes, sir. To begin with it was very complicated, mainly because it appeared to be simple.'

'The court will appreciate the irony of that. However, your investigations soon showed these two deaths were not what they at first appeared to be?'

'There were certain factors that didn't fit. If I may use a phrase, the rhythm of the case became wrong.'

'I'm sure we can understand what you mean by that, Superintendent. Will you tell us what happened?'

'Right from the beginning, I was puzzled by the amount

of cattle cake that was stored in the interior Dutch barn—
if the farm was in such a parlous financial state, why had
Knott spent so much money on buying food at a time when
it was not wanted? Then from the PM I learned that the
contents of the second dead man's stomach showed a meal
far too heavy for a day that was one of the hottest . . .'

He was a smooth bastard, thought Clayton disgustedly,
no shadow of doubt about that.

Riger was a domineering cross-examiner, using a heavy
broadsword rather than a rapier. As he stared at Mrs Knott
in the witness-box, he rested his thumbs in the buttonholes
of his tail coat and spread his hands out over his large
stomach. 'You say your marriage was happy?' he asked in
tones of incredulity.

'It was always happy.' It was obvious she was lying, but
she gained sympathy from the manner in which she faced
him, very afraid yet ready to fight.

'Can you really claim it was happy when you knew your
husband was going around with another woman?'

'He wasn't.'

'You've heard Miss Clews testify that you saw her and
your husband dining in a restaurant.'

'She's lying.'

Riger leaned forward until his stomach was pressed
against the edge of the desk-flap. 'Did your husband ever
spend a night away from home?'

'Yes,' she answered reluctantly. Her hair was in some
disorder, her face was badly lined, and there was no colour
in her cheeks. She looked well into middle age.

'How often would he be away at night?'

'I . . . I can't remember.'

'Did he often leave the farm during the day?'

'Yes, but . . . He had to do business.'

'What business?'

'There was market day and . . . and people to see.'

'What people?'

'I . . . Just people.' She gestured vainly with her hands.

'Is it not true to say that in the last few months of his life your husband spent more time away from the farm than on it?'

'Yes, but . . .' Again the gesture with her hands: a gesture that suggested the vain struggling of a trapped bird.

'Did you know your husband was spending a great deal of money?'

'No.'

'Yet you've admitted that the amount he gave you for housekeeping was cut down in December of last year and again in February?'

'I just thought . . . The farm was doing so badly . . .'

'Your husband was often away from the farm during the day, was sometimes away all night, and he was spending money. Surely, in the face of this evidence, you must have been suspicious he was going out with another woman?'

'I knew he wasn't,' she said loudly.

'What do you mean by that?'

'He was my husband. He was a Knott.'

'He was a Knott,' repeated Riger, with heavy sarcasm. 'Is that supposed to make him incapable of committing adultery?'

'Yes,' she cried.

Riger wearily shrugged his shoulders. 'Where did you go on Monday, the twenty-first of August?'

'My friend, Miss Corrins, picked me up and we went to her home.'

'And your husband stayed at the farm?'

'Yes.'

'What time did you arrive at Miss Corrins's house?'

'It was about ten o'clock.'

'At what time did you leave her house?'

'We didn't leave it until the evening,' she said, more loudly than she had previously spoken.

Riger looked at the jury with an expression of exasperation. 'Mrs Knott, you do your case no good by so obviously lying.'

'I'm not lying.'

'Mr Jarrold has testified that you drove away from Miss Corrins's house at about one-thirty. Miss Clews has testified you were outside the shop where she works at a little after two.'

'They're lying.'

'Mr Jarrold has further testified that he was bribed to say you did not leave the house in the afternoon.'

'He's lying.'

'Why should he lie? What possible motive can he have?' Tears welled out of her eyes.

'I put it to you that it is you who have been lying from the very beginning. You drove away from Miss Corrins's house at about one-thirty and reached Trighton at two. You went to the shop where Miss Clews works and stared at her through the window and the sight of her increased your desperate jealousy of her and hatred for your husband who was deceiving you. You drove back to Knott Farm, where you knew your husband was planning an insurance swindle, and you found him in the act of setting that fraud in motion. You accused him of deceiving you. You grabbed the shotgun off the wall of the store-room . . .'

'No,' she cried.

'You loaded the gun with two cartridges from the box you'd bought with his murder in mind, you aimed the gun, fired, and he crumpled to the ground . . .'

'Oh, God, I swear it wasn't like that.'

'And as he lay there dead, shot by you, you calmly set about making the crime seem a self-contained murder.'

'No,' she screamed. 'I didn't shoot him. I couldn't ever have done, even though I was so desperate. I begged him to give her up, I pleaded with him time after time, but I couldn't ever have killed him.'

'Then you did know your husband was having an affair with Miss Clews?'

She sobbed heavily.

'Did you drive to Trighton and stare at Miss Clews through the shop window?'

'Yes,' she mumbled.

'And you then drove back to Knott Farm?'

She struggled to regain some self-control. 'I never went back to the farm. I just drove round and round . . . I couldn't think what to do . . . I was so desperate . . .' She broke down and wept.

The judge spoke. 'The court will adjourn for ten minutes to help the witness regain her composure.'

'My Lord . . .' began Riger in protest, seemingly oblivious of the very deep distress of the accused.

The judge stood up and left the dais by the right-hand door.

Mrs Knott had regained a measure of composure and her distress was now only immediately obvious from the fact that she could not keep her hands still. Her eyes were red and puffy, but she managed to contain further tears. 'I . . . I tried to find out where Daniel was going and who he was seeing, but he wouldn't tell me. Then one day I went with Pamela to a restaurant at Craxley Green and . . . and saw Daniel with her.' She turned and looked quickly at Hazel Clews, who sat in the centre of a row of seats, and her mouth twisted in bitter hatred.

'What did you do when you saw your husband at this restaurant?' asked Riger.

'I . . . I left immediately.'

'You didn't speak to him?'

'I wasn't going to make a scene.'

'But no doubt there was a scene later that night when your husband returned home?'

She made no answer.

'Did you at that time know who the woman was whom you'd seen with your husband?'

'No.'

'What did you do about this situation?'

'I . . . I tried to find out who she was.'

'Why?'

'I wanted to beg her to leave my husband alone.'

'Did you imagine such an appeal would meet with any success?'

'Can't you understand? I had to try.'

'How did you set about looking for her?'

'Daniel had told me she lived in Trighton when he tried to make me believe she was just the daughter of an old friend. I wandered round the town, looking for her.'

'You wandered round the town in the hopes you'd just bump into her?' said Riger, in tones of disbelief.

'Can't you see,' she said pathetically, 'that I had to try to speak to her?'

'Did you ever catch sight of her?'

'Only once.'

'When was this?'

'I saw her going into Central Station with a man.'

'Not your husband?'

'I don't know who he was.'

'Did you speak to her?'

'I bought a platform ticket and went in, but I chose the wrong platform. She was on the other side for the Parqueton train and by the time I got over there, the train had gone out.'

'When was this?'

'A few days before . . .' She gripped the edge of the witness-box with both hands.

'Before you killed him,' said Riger harshly.

'I didn't kill him,' she shouted.

Riger turned over a page of his notebook. 'What happened on the twenty-first of August to send you suddenly to Trighton?'

'I was at Elizabeth's. There was a telephone call when we were eating and someone told me I'd find Daniel's girl-friend working in a flower-shop called Carol, in Trighton. I drove straight to Trighton and went to the shop. I . . . I saw her inside.'

'Did it upset you to see her?'

'Of course it did.'

'Did you go inside and speak to her?'

'No.'

'Why not?'

'I . . . I wasn't going to make a scene.'

'But you've just told us that you wanted to know who she was to ask her to leave your husband alone.'

'But I couldn't do that in the shop . . . I didn't know what to do. I went back to the car and drove into the hills and tried to work out how to speak to her without making a scene.'

'I put it to you that you did nothing of the sort. Frantic with jealousy, you drove to the farm and shot your husband dead.'

'I couldn't have shot him,' she said desperately. 'Why can't you understand? We were the Knotts.'

Riger was not the man to forgo the obvious retort: 'Your husband was a Knott, yet he had committed murder in order to carry out an insurance fraud.'

She was silent.

Riger thrust his hands into his trouser pockets. 'If you did not murder your husband, why did you bother to try to bribe Mr Jarrold to say you'd never left the house?'

'I didn't want anyone to know I'd been in Trighton searching for the woman. I tried to hide what Daniel had been up to.'

'Why?'

'I've told you. We were the Knotts.'

'You were the Knotts!' he repeated sarcastically. 'Mrs Knott, if you did not shoot your husband, how do you explain the fact that your finger-prints were on the box of Super County cartridges and on some of the cartridges in that box?'

She spoke in so low a voice that many people in the court failed to hear what she said. 'When I got home on Monday, I found a box of cartridges and some loose ones on the small table by the telephone. I just put the loose cartridges in the box and the box in the case in the gun-room.'

'Was this after you'd been told by the police that two men had been found dead in the store-room?'

'Yes.'

'Are you saying that you'd received the most terrible news any married woman could receive and all you could do was tidy up the house?'

'I . . . I didn't know what I was doing . . . I always kept the house tidy and so I tidied these up . . .'

'Incredible behaviour—for an innocent person.'

'I didn't kill him,' she cried.

CHAPTER XIX

CLAYTON SAT at his desk and stared out of the window. It was one of those October mornings when the sky was cloudless, there was little wind, and the air had a champagne sparkle to it almost as if summer lay ahead and not behind.

The trial had been adjourned the previous night and would not now resume until Monday morning. Hapwood would re-examine Mrs Knott, closing speeches would be made, the judge would sum up, and the jury would retire to consider their verdict. There was little doubt what that verdict would be.

He stared at the paper-work which had accumulated since the beginning of the trial, despite all his efforts to clear it. He ought to be dealing with some of it now, but he kept wondering about certain odd facts which had bothered him from the time each came to light. Assume both barrels of the gun had been fired in the store-room at Knott Farm, as the test had suggested, why were three cartridges missing from the box of twenty-five found in Knott's house? 'Alexander' had not been wearing gloves when he left Mrs Wade's, yet the van had not had a fingerprint inside or outside. 'Alexander's' journey need only have taken thirty minutes, yet the van had not driven up to the farm until forty-five minutes after leaving the house . . .

Could you believe Mrs Knott? Could you believe that any woman in the present world would ever set such store by a name? Could you believe that all her thoughts and actions would be controlled by the one overriding desire to conceal anything that might tarnish the name of Knott? He could. That was why it had always seemed to him that her guilt was odd, the first of several breaks in the rhythm of the crime . . .

She had come from humdrum surroundings and had married a man from an ancient family whom she believed to be wealthy: perhaps in her imagination married life was going to consist of luxury hotels, private yachts, gay parties, Monte Carlo, royalty . . . When the years had taught her the bitter truth, she had been left with nothing but the name. She clung frantically to that, finding in it something which to anyone else had long since been lost. She was a woman who had lived for and by an illusion, even at a time when that illusion had been shattered. She had known her husband was utterly careless of his name and was having an affair, yet she had done everything possible to prevent that affair becoming common knowledge for fear the name of Knott would become tarnished. In her world, a Knott could not murder, even though a Knott had murdered.

M

Suppose she had told all the truth and nothing but the truth? She had arrived home that Monday to discover her husband was almost certainly dead. In her shock—and perhaps some grief, because her husband would still be the romantic aristocrat she had married as well as the man who had betrayed her—she had acted automatically and had tidied up the house, her bitter frustration having resulted in her developing a mania for tidiness. She had seen the cartridges and the box by the telephone, had put the cartridges into the box and the box into the case in the gun-room.

The murderer had shot Daniel Knott with a size 3 shot, a box of which cartridges had been brought to the farm. But anyone who'd visited the farm and been in the store-room would have known that in there was a gun, old but still in working order, and cartridges. Therefore, the murderer had never been in the store-room. Only Hazel Clews and Alf Shear would never have been in there.

Hazel Clews would have known all the details of the proposed insurance swindle—those she wasn't willingly told by Knott, she'd have wheedled out of him. She'd passed the news on to Shear, who'd found the forty thousand pounds irresistible. She wasn't stupid, but Shear was far smarter than she. He'd realized there was a chance to kill Knott and make his death appear the result of a fight with Alexander, the non-existent commercial traveller. Shear had even been able to visualize the possibility that the police might discover these two deaths were not an 'enclosed' murder and so had gone on to plan that in such eventuality suspicion must fall on Mrs Knott.

Four people had been suspects, three had had good alibis for the time of death : logically, this made the fourth person the murderer. But if one tackled the problem the other way round and said Mrs Knott was not the murderer, but had been drawn to Trighton in order to make certain she did not have an alibi, what then? Obviously, the time of death had to be wrong.

Browland had been quite sure there had been no shot between ten past two, when he left his house, and five past three. The van had driven up to the farm at a quarter past two. But weren't there three cartridges missing from the box, and hadn't the van taken forty-five minutes to do a thirty-minute journey, and hadn't the van been wiped clear of prints . . .? Knott had had to make his departure from Mrs Wade seem a perfectly normal one, so he'd not cleaned the van down before he drove off, nor had he worn gloves. But because the van had to be free of his prints, he'd stopped somewhere reasonably near to the farm where he could park the van out of sight and wipe it clear. He'd been doing this when he'd been shot—with the third cartridge. The time? About five past two—which gave Shear plenty of time to drive over from the pub in Trighton, which he and Hazel Clews had left at about ten past one. The sound of the shot? Browland hadn't left his house until ten past two and in any case, if the van had been a mile or so away from the farm and to the north of it, he'd not have heard the sound even if he'd been outside. As for anyone else's noticing the shot, guns were fired so frequently in the countryside, and so many explosive bird scarers were in use, that this one would not have aroused any comment in the mind of anyone—except a poacher!—who did hear it, even in retrospect, since it was well away from the murder farm and had been fired an hour before the murder was believed to have been committed. Shear had put the body in the van and had driven to the farm. At the beginning, it had been assumed that Alexander had been at the wheel of the van as it went up the farm drive, then, when it was discovered there was no such person as Alexander, it had automatically been accepted the driver was Knott. But there'd never been any proof of this. The landlord of the local pub had been quite unable to identify him.

Shear had been back in Trighton at twenty past three, which meant he'd left the farm buildings at about two thirty-five, had had ten minutes to walk to wherever he'd left his own vehicle, thirty minutes to drive to Trighton, and five minutes to park and get to the flower-shop.

When the shot in the store-room had been fired and the fire had started, Shear had been half-way back to Trighton, so there must have been some sort of timing mechanism. Clayton remembered the two small fused lumps of brass that had been sifted from the ashes—brass eye-screws or cup hooks through which string had been threaded?

He stood up, turned, and went over to the bookcase and brought out of it a forensic text-book. In the chapter on arson, there were descriptions of the more common types of mechanical and chemical time-fuses. Mechanical fuses were subject to the evil of all mechanical things—they could break down : chemical fuses were far more reliable. The list of popular chemical compounds was short—phosphorus dissolved in disulphide of carbon, sulphuric acid, potassium chlorate, and powdered sugar, phosphide of calcium, metallic sodium, and metallic potassium. The text described the use of these chemicals and stated that the simplest time-fuse was made by suspending a bottle of sulphuric acid over the potassium chlorate mixture. The bottle was sealed with a thin cork or thick paper, the acid ate through the sealer, dripped down on to the mixture, and then started a violent fire.

He began to draw on paper, trying to work out the possible way in which the gun had been fired and the fire started. For a time his drawings were highly complicated, then he realized that the simplest way was by far the best and that this called for two cup hooks. A weight was suspended by running string through a cup hook and securing the end of the string. A second length of string, slack, was taken from the weight on the opposite side and up to an eye hook and then down to the gun and made fast to the triggers. The bottle of sulphuric acid was tied to the first, and taut, string and the potassium mixture was placed directly underneath. When the acid dripped down, a violent fire started. The string was burned through. The weight came on to the second string and the jerk fired both triggers . . .

He lit a cigarette. Theorizing with the aid of known facts was one thing, proving the theory was another. How to prove Shear and Hazel Clews had murdered Knott? He remembered something. At the trial, Mrs Knott had broken down and eventually confessed she had seen the two of them get on to the Parqueton train only a few days before the murder: wouldn't they normally have taken great care not to be seen together before the murder and didn't this journey therefore probably mean it had had something to do with their plans?

Clayton jerked himself upright in the chair and used the internal phone to speak to Morris. 'George, I want those mug shots of Alf Shear we had.'

'Right, sir, I'll see if we can find them.'

Clayton reached across his desk for the morning's copy of the *Daily Express*. On one of the inside pages was a report of the trial and a photo of Hazel Clews. He cut out the photo with a pair of scissors. He spoke to Burrows over the phone and told him he was to accompany him to Parqueton.

Morris came into the room and handed him a copy of the official photograph of Alf Shear. 'I'm off to Parqueton with Burrows,' Clayton said. He indicated the papers on his desk. 'Deal with them, will you?'

'I've a lot of work . . .' began Morris.

'Now you've got a lot more.' Clayton picked up his mackintosh and hurried out of the room.

After a quick word with the divisional superintendent of B division to say they were in the other's territory, Clayton and Burrows began their boring and wearying task: Clayton to question the staff of ironmongers, chemists, and gunsmiths, Burrows to question stores which dealt in the luxury trades. Neither had to remind himself of the odds against success. Hazel Clews and Shear might have got off at one of the five stations before Parqueton, or have travelled to any of the seven beyond : this might not have been the trip on which they bought the tools they needed for the murder : some of the things they might have bought would be so ordinary that no shop assistant could be expected to remember their being bought. Yet, knowing this, both worked on patiently, endlessly.

Parqueton, a cathedral town, was very crowded. Records from the Middle Ages referred to the narrow, crooked streets filled to overflowing with honest pilgrims and the rogues who preyed on them—today, pavements were solid with pedestrians, the roads with cars. Shop assistants were overworked and frequently ill-tempered. 'Cup hooks? Do I remember selling some cup hooks to those two in the photos? Have you any idea how many cup hooks I sell in a week? How do you expect me . . .' or too eager to help, 'Isn't she the girl who was going out with the man who was murdered and whose wife did it? I'm sure I've seen her. I said so to Viv. No, I can't remember what she bought and . . .' or else were just unable to help, 'No, I've sold no cartridges to either of them.'

At four-fifteen Clayton found himself outside a tea-shop. He disliked such places on principle, unjustly claiming they were all run by refugees from South Kensington, but he went in. He ordered bread and jam, cakes, and coffee. He ate all the bread and jam, and the cakes, and had three cups of coffee although it tasted vaguely nasty.

Refreshed, he resumed his work, pushing his way through crowds which even seemed to have grown in volume, questioning assistants who became less and less helpful as they grew tireder. He stopped in front of a library and lit a cigarette. His feet were hot and aching and he was beginning to feel really tired. He sighed at the thought that his present discomfort was all of his own making, walked on, and entered a do-it-yourself shop, filled with everything any handyman could need. He explained to the owner what he wanted and passed the photos across.

The owner was completely bald, with a very high-domed head, large ears, and a pair of horn-rimmed spectacles. He fingered his round chin. 'I've seen her,' he said.

'Can you be certain?' asked Clayton excitedly, suddenly no longer feeling tired.

'Yes, I can.'

'Have you any idea when it was?'

He puffed out his cheeks. 'That's difficult.'

A woman came into the shop and asked for the set of chair-legs her husband had ordered. The owner served her. When he returned to where Clayton stood, he said: 'It was just before I went on holiday—maybe one week, maybe two.'

'So when does that place it?'

'The beginning or the middle of August.'

'Was this bloke with her?'

'He was.'

'Can you remember what they bought?'

'I can indeed. They wanted two cup hooks. I offered 'em a packet of a dozen and they said they only wanted two and the others would be wasted. I told 'em I only bought them in packets these days.'

'What happened?'

'I opened a packet and sold 'em two. It's no good turning away customers—even the likes of them.'

Thank God for meanness, thought Clayton. If they'd been content to buy ten more cup hooks than they were going to need for the murder, they'd not have been remembered.

After taking a statement, he left the shop and stood on the pavement. It was reasonable to suppose they'd bought the other things near by and he saw there was a chemist on the cross-roads.

He went into the chemist's and spoke to the dispenser, a

middle-aged man with the drawn, pinched expression of someone for whom life had always been a struggle.

The dispenser examined the photographs with care. He shook his head. 'Can't say I remember them.'

'They'd have bought something that would start a pretty fierce fire,' said Clayton. 'Possibly some kind of phosphorus.'

'Practically all phosphorus compounds are on schedule one of the poisons list so they'd have to have had authorization and to sign the poisons register.'

Clayton shook his head. 'They wouldn't have done that. What about potassium chlorate and sulphuric acid? Would you sell anyone those two?'

'Not together, not unless I knew the person well.'

'What about one on its own?'

'I'd do that if the person could persuade me he wanted it for a legitimate reason.'

'Would that be difficult?'

'Not really, I suppose,' said the dispenser reluctantly.

'Can you remember selling either sulphuric acid or potassium chlorate to anyone back in August?'

The dispenser shook his head. 'It's a long time ago and . . .' He stopped.

'Well?'

'There's something at the back of my mind. Someone came in . . . He wanted sulphuric acid and I offered him a small bottle and he said he didn't want so much . . .' He turned and called to one of the two assistants. 'Betty, come over here, will you?'

Betty was a girl of eighteen made up to look at least five years older. 'What's up, Mr Potter?' she asked.

'D'you remember someone coming in here and asking for sulphuric acid and when I offered a small bottle he only wanted a quarter of that, so I had to go to all the trouble of finding a container with a safe top?'

She shook her head. 'Can't say I do.'

Clayton showed her the photographs.

She giggled. 'There's that lovely man!'

'What?' said the dispenser.

She giggled louder. 'Real mean—with eyes like that, he'd be exciting!' She suddenly looked up. 'Here, it was him what wanted the acid. I remember now.' She studied the photo again. 'Isn't he sharp?' She sighed. 'My Bert's nothing like him.'

'And a very good job, too,' snapped the dispenser.

Clayton questioned her closely, but learned little more. The 'exciting' man had been with a woman, but she couldn't remember her at all. They'd been the ones who bought the acid all right, because Mr Potter had been furious as it had taken so long to find something to put the acid into . . .

Clayton left. He visited the other chemists in the area, but none of them particularly remembered selling any potassium chlorate. Shops began to close, a few minutes early in most cases, and he battled his way through the crowds to his parked car. As he lit a cigarette, Burrows approached.

'Any luck?' asked Clayton, as the other opened the front passenger door.

Burrows got in and sat down. He took a notebook from his pocket. 'I went into a furrier's called Terrence—down Pembroke Lane—and they recognized Hazel Clews. She'd been in and tried on some fur coats, including a mink at sale price. She said she wanted the mink but couldn't pay for it until the end of the month or the beginning of September and would the shop keep it for her. She never went back. She bought and took away two large plastic bags—the kind fur coats are sometimes hung up in.'

Clayton smoked. The plastic bags had been used to store Knott's body in from the place where he was shot to the farm. There was now some proof of intention and means of commission, but the proof wasn't strong. The brass cup hooks could have been bought for a dozen and one reasons, the sulphuric acid was needed for a battery, the mink was ordered in a rush of unwarranted optimism, the plastic bags were to protect two ordinary coats . . . If only there were some way of proving Hazel Clews had known all about the insurance swindle and the forty thousand to which she was the beneficiary, in direct contradiction to the evidence she had given in court . . .

'I wonder!' he suddenly said aloud.

Clayton spoke over the telephone to the assistant chief constable for the eastern area.

'Why are you asking me to put this request through to the French police?' asked the ACC. 'You're not in charge of the case.'

'No, sir.'

'And so far as we're concerned, this case is now over?'

'Yes, sir.'

'Then any such request is, to say the least, unusual and must come through Detective-Superintendent Akers.'

Clayton hesitated. 'Sir,' he said suddenly.

'Well, what is it?'

'Superintendent Akers isn't likely to agree to asking you.'

'Then I fail utterly to understand why you've telephoned me.'

'It seemed the only thing to do. Unfortunately, Superintendent Akers believes the county police are a bunch of hicks and that anything they suggest is bound to be stupid.'

The ACC's voice became still more clipped. 'What makes you say that?'

'He's told me several times that the county police are capable of investigating chicken thefts, but it needs the experts from London to cope with anything more serious.'

'I see. Then perhaps we should take the opportunity to convince him otherwise. I'll forward your request to the French police. You will want to travel there yourself, of course?'

'Yes, sir. I wonder if Superintendent Barry should be told?'

'I'll inform him that I've authorized the trip.'

'Thank you, sir.'

'I hope you're right in all you've said.' The ACC's voice was not without a note of warning.

Clayton had no idea that the Hotel Corniche rated two stars in the Guide Michelin and when the manager of the hotel, on his arrival there Monday morning with Inspector Augremy, offered lunch in a private room while they waited, he mentally envisaged something in the order of an omelette and, perhaps, a carafe of wine. How wrong he was was proved when he was offered a menu of truly Lucullan proportions. He was openly perplexed by the magnificence of choice. The manager and Inspector Augremy tried to advise him and then began to argue, becoming quite heated: the manager said a visiting Englishman should have *Timbale de langouste au porto*, whilst the inspector was equally insistent that only *cochon de lait de Beaune mode des vendages* was suitable to the occasion.

After lunch, eaten in the manager's small sitting-room which adjoined the office, and after he had drunk the last drop of fine champagne, Inspector Augremy settled back in one of the two easy arm-chairs, closed his eyes, and apparently fell asleep at once. Hardly the proper way to keep watch, thought Clayton. If an English detective-inspector were to sleep on duty, surely an inconceivable event, there would be hell to pay . . .

The telephone awoke him with a start. Inspector Augremy grunted twice and then opened his eyes, reached across to the small table and the receiver. He spoke briefly in French, replaced the receiver, and said in his heavily accented but easily understood English: 'She is arrived. She is with the manager.'

They went through to the office. Hazel Clews sat in front of the desk and when she turned and saw Clayton she drew in her breath with a sharp gasp.

'Good afternoon, Miss Clews,' he said formally.

'What . . . what are you doing here?' she muttered.

'Surely that's obvious?'

She struggled to regain her composure. 'I don't understand.'

'A letter was sent to you telling you that certain papers had been posted to this hotel a few days before the twenty-first of August, to await the arrival of a person who had booked a double room for three weeks. That person never arrived and the papers were opened to see if they appeared to be important. Your name and address was the only one to appear and you were asked if you could say what was to be done with them. Is that correct?'

'Well?' she demanded shrilly. 'All I've done is come here to collect Daniel's papers.'

'By coming here, you've furnished the last link in the chain proving you helped murder him.'

'That's a lie,' she shouted.

'You rushed here because you were scared those papers might incriminate you.'

'No.'

'You'd double-crossed him. That left you wide open to fearing he might have foreseen this possibility and tried to guard against it, despite his wild infatuation for you. You came here to see if you'd been named as a full accomplice in the insurance swindle.'

'I didn't know of the swindle. I never knew about the life insurance.'

'How did you know to come to this hotel?' he asked.

'I told you, they wrote me.'

'The letter informed you that the room had been booked in the name of Fergusson. How could you have known Fergusson was Knott?'

She desperately sought an answer. 'I hadn't any idea who Fergusson was. They just said there were some papers here with my name and address in them.'

'A moment ago, you told us you'd come here to collect Daniel's papers, yet I very carefully never named the writer of them.'

For a moment, she could not hide her panic. Then she said: 'All right. When we stayed at hotels, that's what he said our name was.'

'This booking began the night of the twenty-first and was for three weeks. Neither Mrs Knott, nor anyone else, had any idea he was leaving the country.'

'I didn't know he was coming to France.'

'Or to this hotel?'

'How could I know that?'

'You'd absolutely no idea?'

'How many more times do I have to tell you I hadn't?'

He spoke slowly. 'Then how did you know which hotel to come to today?'

'The letter told me.'

'The letter was written on unheaded notepaper and posted in Boulogne.'

She appeared to shiver.

'In court, you swore on oath you knew nothing of the insurance swindle—yet you could only have arrived here today if you'd known all about it. You and Shear arranged the murder of Daniel Knott, who was shot when he was cleaning off the prints from the van. Shear did the actual killing after you'd fed him with all the information he needed to set up the murder. When the gun in the storeroom fired at five past three, set off by the time-fuse that also fired the building, you were in the shop and as Shear came and spoke to you fifteen minutes later it seemed clear neither of you could have had anything to do with the murder. You might have got away with it if that box of three shot cartridges hadn't been left in the house to try to incriminate Mrs Knott, if there hadn't been three instead of two cartridges missing from the box—by the way, what happened to the gun Shear took there, the murder weapon, not knowing he'd find one on the place?—if the van hadn't taken forty-five minutes to do a thirty-minute journey; if, once it was clear we no longer believed the murders to be enclosed ones, you hadn't deliberately told me Mrs Knott knew about your affair; if you hadn't ordered a mink coat which you never collected from Terrence in Parqueton and bought two very large bags to shove Knott's body into; and if you hadn't been so mean as to refuse to buy more cup hooks or sulphuric acid than you actually needed to carry out the murder.'

She shook her head frantically.

'You're lucky,' he said, speaking slowly. 'You helped plan the murder, but it seems at the moment that you didn't take an active part in it—if that's really true, you'll get off more lightly than Shear, who'll be given a life sentence.'

He had not misjudged her character. Shown a way of partial escape, she took it. It had been Shear's idea from the moment she'd first mentioned Knott's proposed plans. But for him, she'd never have thought of such a horrible thing . . .

Pretty soon, thought Clayton, he ought to take some notice of the judges' rules and caution her.

Riger often became caught up in, and entranced by, his own rhetoric: it happened in his closing speech and he was in the middle of an involved mixed metaphor—which left the jury bewildered—when his instructing solicitor tugged the back of his gown. Angrily, he turned and was about to express his feelings when his instructing solicitor spoke in a low voice.

After a minute, the judge said: 'Mr Riger, are you intending to continue?'

He turned. 'My Lord, something of the utmost importance has come to hand. I am informed that the police have uncovered fresh evidence that is quite vital to this case.'

There was a rising murmur of voices which a call from the usher silenced. 'It is very late in the day to hear new evidence, Mr Riger.'

'Quite so, my Lord, but with respect it is essential that this evidence be heard.'

The judge leaned back in his chair. 'Very well.'

'Detective-Superintendent Akers,' said Riger.

Akers, clearly for once in a state of bewilderment, slowly rose to his feet.

'Come along,' snapped Riger.

Akers made his way into the witness-box. 'I'm very much afraid . . .' he began.

Riger interrupted him. 'You've been sworn, Superintendent, so you're still on oath. Please tell the court what this new evidence is.'

'But . . . but I've no idea.'

'What's that?' asked the judge severely.

Akers spoke almost wildly. 'My Lord, I . . . I just don't know . . .'

'This is quite monstrous. We are told the police have uncovered fresh evidence that is vital, yet the senior police witness confesses he knows nothing of it. Mr Riger, how do you explain this?'

Riger, gesticulating a great deal, once more spoke to his instructing solicitor. He turned back. 'My Lord, I understand that the evidence has only just come to hand and there's been no time to inform Mr Akers of it. Detective-Inspector Clayton is only this moment back from France . . .'

'Does he know anything about what's going on?'

'Yes, my Lord.'

'Perhaps we should be thankful that one of the policemen

investigating the case does. Put him in the box, then. Let's waste no more time on recalling witnesses who know nothing.'

Clayton took Akers's place in the witness-box.

Riger spoke angrily. 'What new evidence is to hand, Inspector?'

'May I start, sir, by explaining that from the beginning there've been several odd factors that worried me, breaks in the rhythm of the crime . . .'

'Well, love?' asked Margery, as Clayton stepped into the hall.

'Akers called me a lot of very rude names,' he replied.

She kissed him. 'Poor devil. He really shouldn't have stepped outside his class.'